Our Better Nature

A Collection of Five Christmas Stories

Darrell W. McNabb

PAGE PUBLISHING, INC.
New York, NY

First originally published by Page Publishing, Inc. 2018

ISBN 978-1-64214-310-2 (Paperback)
ISBN 978-1-64214-311-9 (Digital)

Printed in the United States of America

To my friends April & Chloe,
may this book both inspire
and God bless you.
Darrell

To my family and friends I dedicate this work, and with it I give you the best part of me. And I cannot launch this book without acknowledging my friend, Bill Manning, for his faith in my writing, and his continuing support and encouragement, both in this life and beyond it.

The Woman and the One-Armed Man

Sentiment without action is the ruin of the soul.
—Edward Abbey

To many she is just another unfortunate soul, and like so much litter, she is swept to the side of the great social highway—a retarded mongoloid woman all of fifty years old—nobody's hero. She talks to herself and shuffles along the street with seemingly aimless intention. On an unbecoming face, she wears an unwitting expression and heavy glasses, and through lenses that are the thickness of Coke bottles, she views a cold and hostile world racing by her. She is not pretty, and her clothes are worn and don't match. She is simpleminded and may be easily perceived by others who don't know her as a dumb, meaningless creature and most certainly not worth their time. But of all her many faults and failures to even come close to the standards that society has chosen to heap upon this woman, she is most guilty of her compassion for others—you see, she is at fault for wearing her heart about her neck. While she may fall well short of fitting in and her silent comings and goings (e.g., her purpose), covered up by the seeming importance of the affairs others, she will not remain buried underneath the business as usual in crowd, and I will raise her estate with the ink of my pen as she, who may be short in stature, becomes the charitable hero of this story by refusing to be the victim.

Now it is commonly known that, not unlike gambling houses and 7-Elevens, the ever-open-for-business Laundromat never sleeps and remains busy servicing the many needy patrons who feed the hungry machines day and night, weekends and holidays. Oh yes, one could wait and show up at some unusual time or ungodly hour with the intention of missing the rush, and alas, you would find that everyone else had the same idea—no, you would have to learn to wait, to be patient, to share. I, for one, not wanting to miss this opportunity to indulge my favorite pastime of people-watching, would show up at the busiest of times just to satisfy my curiosity about the Laundromat dynamics.

It was a good place to watch everyday people go about their ordinary, uninteresting, mundane affair of laundering their clothes. You watched them while they watched you, as each in turn would break the ranks, step up from their waiting roost on the sidelines—called upon by their washing machines and driers, which were uniformly stacked and lined up in rows throughout the building—and absorb themselves in loading and unloading, sorting, measuring, pouring, and folding. It is woman's work, to which I answer, no, sir, it is not—the surprising number of men who frequent the place can attest to that.

To me it was the ultimate social experiment of which I was a part. It was my schoolhouse where I soaked up the opportunity to study and experience the interactions of everyday people brought together at a common place, bound by a common purpose. Again, I was privileged to learn many things about the nature of people, who, like the variety of clothes and colors they brought with them, were all thrown into the mix together. They were as diverse and distant from each other as the earth is from the moon. There were rich and poor, young and old, smart and dull, pretty and plain alike—a cross section of gender, culture, and race—and the doors opened to everyone, and no one was turned away. Some were fastidious, some were slobs, some had heaping piles of dirty clothes, and another might have a single pair of socks. And some others would remove the clothes they wore and wash them while they stood by in the buff, and they all arrived toting their bags and tubs of clothes, soaps, softeners, sacks, and hangers, and collected under one roof and for one purpose.

One can spend hours with their eyes trained on the night sky in order to capture that one shooting star, that spectacular moment of discovery of a thing hoped for and seldom seen, and in just this way, I was about to be rewarded again for my patience and perseverance. For out of all my observations and for all the time I spent searching this human landscape at the Laundromat, there were occasionally highlights, that one exceptional occurrence that stood out from the rest and begged me to write about it—this is one of those events.

On this day, there entered three mentally retarded middle-aged mongoloid ladies who always came together on laundry day. They were not unknown to the area, a familiar sight in this, our part of town as I had seen them before many times walking down the street in a line, resembling a family of ducklings in descending order, push-ing their shopping carts full of laundry in all kinds of weather—in the rain they covered up with plastic garbage bags, and in the sun they wore sweaters and hats. One would easily find them follow-ing the familiar path, not unlike the rest of us; they were creatures of habit. Familiar people made weekly trips to the Laundromat and the adjacent grocery store. You could set your watch by the predict-able patterns of people—they had their routine, and we had ours. I watched as the three took care of one another and fussed over each other as they went about their business of washing, drying, and fold-ing their clothes. And who would have thought that this day would be different from any other day at the Laundromat.

Now it just so happened that also on this day, a well-dressed, professional-looking man whom I didn't recognize was standing at one of the folding tables, and not without some slight difficulty, he was patiently folding his expensive white dress shirts. It was not the man himself that necessarily interested me or caught my attention, but clearly I was intrigued by the technique he was forced to imple-ment in order to fold his clothes, considering he had but one arm, or rather the lack of one arm. I was amazed at the dexterity of his remaining limb, and I respected his ability as opposed to his disabil-ity; I reflected on the trouble I had in the area of folding as I often struggled with two hands to achieve the standards held to me by my wife—I guess in a way I was happy she was not present at the time to witness what this man could do, lest she elevate her expectation of me.

Now, I wasn't the only one who had noticed this man's short-comings. Along with some other launderers in the gallery stealing glances, and a few menacing children who stared on as if he were a freak in some circus sideshow, the three mongoloid ladies were tuned into him as well.

Just as the man was about to finish folding his last shirt, he lost his grip and it fell to the floor, and as things often go, when he leaned over to pick it up, he inadvertently swept the other shirts, which had all been folded and neatly stacked, off the table and onto the floor as well. He must have been practiced in taking it in stride as he man-aged to disguise his frustration by exhibiting a cool however artificial indifference—I was frustrated for him. He stood there with that "I can't believe I did it again" look on his face.

I watched the one-armed man as the unruly children, who had been running about the place unabated, stopped in front of him, pointed out the obvious absence of his arm, and I further suspect, made fun of his folding foible. They laughed as they darted in the direction of their mother, who was loudly hailing from her post by a drier she was loading with her youngest attached to her hip, "You kids get over here, now!" Like a fisherman who casts his net and rakes in his catch, the woman extended a long arm and proceeded to sweep the arriving children closely into her. Now gathered around the clothes basket in front of her, in sort of a huddle, she further admonished in a voice loud enough for the one-armed man to hear, attempting to override their excited interruptions in order to pass onto their mother the discovery of the one-armed man, "I know . . . I know. Now listen to me, kids. Don't tease the cripple. That's not nice." The man pretended not to notice them.

It is not so much that the one-armed man was so unusual; he wasn't. It was the way in which people reacted to him. In general he was an oddity, just like the three odd-looking ladies, who, by the way, had continued to endure the taunting and teasing of the children since they had stepped into this out-of-control kiddy cauldron. Children, who are curious and candid by nature, can be contentious and cruel on one hand and kind and caring on the other. They will laugh at someone in pain and pour out tears of sympathy at the same time, and to understand this is to understand the simple, uncomplicated nature of children, for children are living paradoxes.

I need you to know that I could very well have helped the man and admonished the children; however, I was not meant to interfere, as we all have a time to act and a time to observe. It was my time to observe and allow what was about to happen unfold.

Now the eldest of the mongoloid ladies had been staring at the man since she arrived. She witnessed the insensitive antics of the children and felt for him, and it came to a point where she could no longer hold back and was motivated to act when she saw the man experience the folding fumble. The lady, driven by her empathetic nature, quickly waddled over to the table next to the man to set things right and make it all better as it were. She just sort of moved in and took over (I mean helped him out) as she folded her short, squat frame in half, scooped the shirts up off the floor with her stubby little arms, and hoisted them up onto the table, which was nearly as tall as she was. Without speaking, she began to refold and neatly stack the shirts, which the man had permitted, only after a slight, albeit artificial, protest. The man in turn faced her and acknowledged her help with a simple thank you.

Upon accomplishing the task, the woman paused and took a long look at the space his arm should have occupied. She then looked deeply into his eyes and in a most pitiful way said to him, "You don't have your arm," as if revealing to him a significant detail concerning his person that he had previously neglected to realize. He agreed and tritely answered, "No, I don't." With the innocence of a child, she further inquired, "I'm sorry, does it hurt? Did you lose your arm? Where did you leave it?" Not allowing the man to respond, the woman thought further on how she could fix his problem. She offered in a voice of growing concern, "We can look for it. I can help you find it. My friends can help too," indicating her companions who were looking on with interest. He studied her face, and noticing her faltering voice and the tears that began to form in her eyes, he calmly assured, "It's okay, really, look I have another," as he gently placed his one hand on her trembling hand. He continued, "It's a small inconvenience, and I can still use it," which he displayed as he reached over, scooped up one of his folded shirts, and cradled it with the stump of his arm, which terminated just beyond his elbow; it had become his makeshift hand.

Still somewhat unconvinced, she ultimately offered, "You can have one of mine." Still trying to console her, the man continued, "You see, it's okay, it still works." He demonstrated again as he inadvertently dropped the shirt he had been cradling with his stub. He paused, shrugged his shoulders, and surrendered as she poured pity into his eyes.

He began, "I lost my arm a long time ago . . . but it's ok now, really."

"You lost your arm," she sadly repeated, and at that moment, she threw herself into him, wrapping him up with her short, stubby arms, patting his back; and with her head tightly buried in his chest, she repeated again, "You lost your arm. I'm sorry. It's all right, because I love you anyway."

He responded to her overwhelming display of compassion and hugged her back, and his eyes became wet and glistened. He looked beyond her, and his eyes fixed on mine.

She finally released her grip on him and backed up slowly, looking at him, and with a calm and complete understanding, she assured him. "It's all right, you're okay. You're doing the best you can," she encouraged. I know that he could not speak because he was overcome with emotion by this outpouring of concern for his welfare. He only managed a smile and a nod in agreement, lest he reduce himself and openly weep in front of all these people who had witnessed this exchange of humanity. Satisfied with her endeavor to reduce the impact that the loss of this man's arm had on his life, she rejoined her companions at their camp by the common table. She watched the man as he thoughtfully collected his shirts and softly spoke an audible thought, "I think I'll go, and put these away." Upon leaving, the man hesitated at the door, turned and looked directly at the woman, smiled, and mouthed the words "Thank you . . . I love you too."

I suggest that even beyond a random act of kindness and caring, more than a simple embrace was exchanged here, that something much more profound occurred between these two souls. I suggest that the woman's words went much deeper and meant much more to the one-armed man than we imagine, that perhaps, just beneath the surface of what we saw there stirred the rest of the story, the greater story, a spiritual story—a Christmas story.

With a viselike grip, this simple yet complex woman held the moment hostage for me and a few others who had been riveted by this event. The power of this woman to impact this moment was amazing, and her emotional generosity overwhelmed me. I sat and pondered the occurrence as my tears evaporated and my focus on what I had witnessed slowly blurred. My drifting attention once again returned, and I became aware of the other activities continuing to occur around me, there in the midst of the laughter of the children playing in the background—and it was like nothing profound had occurred, curious.

As I write this account down, I pause and glance down at my nimble hand, and with a newfound sobriety, I think about the one-armed man and how, in the midst of living with it, he had displayed so much grace—how much I take for granted.

I further think about the benevolent beauty of the woman who had touched me with her simple act of kindness; I cannot imagine a world where she was not, for she is the essence of all that is good in this realm. And I consider all the opportunities I have missed in my life to positively affect someone else's, even in the smallest of ways.

(by Darrell W. McNabb, 2012)

The Angel in the Garden

L et me first submit that the following tale is extraordinary, and had I not lived it myself, I would have doubtless been stayed by the firm hand of unbelief, which, up to that point in my life, steadfastly held me accountable to reason and practicality. There is, between the realm of life and death, a whimsical place where light and shadows delicately dance, and sometimes they seek to interfere in the affairs of the living, altering the path of our lives, which are otherwise founded by fate, drawn by destiny, and directed by design. And for the first time in my young life I knew that there was so much more to this grand and wonderful mystery we call life. I once had faith only in what I could see and touch. I am now challenged to accept that there are transitional elements and events at work here that I may not yet comprehend, understand, or adequately explain.

On a worn and weathered stone bench amidst a large grove of aspen trees, the two sat, pressed together. For the better part of a day, they tarried and bathed in the warmth of each other's company, absorbed in the serenity of the cemetery, where the fanciful spirits of past generations moved in and around them. Like a quiet storm, the concert of aspen leaves shivered, rustled, and released from their branches, announcing the coming of the fall. Upon the stone-studded landscape, covered with a blanket of golden teardrop leaves, lights and shadows danced. Following the rays of light up from the forest floor, she looked up through the dancing trees moved by the wind, and she remembered. A little voice demanded, "Grandma . . . ? Grandma?"

"Yes, little one?"

"I thought you were going to read me the story." Finally capturing her grandmother's attention, and now locked onto her eyes, Raven implored, "Please, Grandma, remember you said."

Grandma looked down at her granddaughter lovingly and recalled, "I was a little older than you are now." She laid her hand on her granddaughter's head and gently stroked her raven-black hair, while her other hand divided the cover of the book resting in her lap, and from the first page, she began to read. "Once upon a time . . ."

Our story takes place in the little town of Kings Landing, which lay in a hidden valley deep in the Rocky Mountains, on the edge of creation. Next to the cemetery, in the very center of a large overgrown piece of land, there stood a stone mansion of monolithic proportion. The massive house, which was set off in the distance, was barely visible from the street as it was surrounded by a thick stand of stately trees, wrapped by tall hedges and lavish gardens overflowing with every conceivable plant, bush, and flower. A tall black spiked wrought iron fence further prevented intrusion. The gate, which opened to a long winding cobblestone driveway, was immense, framed by two columns of granite. Upon the gate was a large black iron piece fashioned in the letter *B* in old English design, which had been permanently affixed to the ornate bars. The place had an air of foreboding—from the leaded glass eyes of the mansion towers, which looked out from above, overlooking the sprawling grounds, to the menacing gargoyles watching from their perch atop of the stone pinnacles at the entrance. Now the meaning of the *B* that hung on the front gate was not lost to the public at large, and while it may have the first letter of *Batton*, the owners' last name, it spoke loudly to all standing before it: "Beware."

"Grandma, *B* stands for *big* too," Raven contributed.

"Yes, little one, you are right, it was very, very BIG."

Of course Constance had known the place existed, yet she knew nothing about its inhabitants or its history that was nothing beyond the local town gossip.

"But, Grandma, your name is Constance," Raven observed excitedly.

"Yes, little one, that is my name . . . and Grandma of course."

"I didn't know you were in the book, Grandma."

"We all have books written about our lives. You and I are writing a book as we speak."

"You mean right now?"

"Yes, Raven, at this very moment, you and I are writing a book, and you know what?"

"What?"

"One day, a long time from now, you will be reading the book you wrote during your life."

Raven looked deeply into her grandmother's eyes and, feeling tingly all over, snuggled in as close to her grandma as she could, looked back at the book, and anxiously waited for the telling of the rest of the story. Constance continued to read.

*　　*　　*

Over the years, it was the incidental path to some other destination that had inadvertently taken Constance by the old place and beyond it. Up to that time, she had not taken notice, and she had no reason to. However, as she got older, between her friends' promotion of the place and her piquing interest, she felt it was time for a visit. Constance now needed to close on the odd and unusual stories she had heard about the place, for it was one of the oldest, most talked about and misunderstood places left standing in the old town. And so it was, that on a cool autumn day . . . much like this day, accompanied by two of her friends, she went to see the old Batton place for the first time. Constance had no idea that this one afternoon's excursion was about to change the direction of her entire life.

While Constance dwelled and wondered in front of the old house, her friends pressed, "Hurry, Constance, come on."

Abby pulled her along. "You can't let her see you."

"My mom would kill me if she knew," Denise added.

"Mine too," Abby agreed.

"Wait, do you see it, up high in the attic window? I think it's a girl standing there," and as if reconfirming to herself, Constance repeated, "There's a girl standing in that window." Constance insisted as she broke free of the grip Abby had on her hand and pointed. "Up there . . . see it?"

"I know, just like I said," Denise confirmed and directed. "Okay, you saw it, can we go now?"

Constance just stood in place, not moving, and continued to stare at the image. Her two companions, who had gone ahead of her, ran back to Constance, grabbed her hand, and pulled her along. Constance continued to look up at the image in the window, afraid that if she looked away, she would disappear.

Finally getting her attention, Denise offered, "You know that a witch lives there?" Constance was suspicious. Denise reinforced, "No, really."

Constance spoke, "I don't believe in witches. I'm sure there's an explanation."

"Well, maybe you should," Denise added and went on to sell the thought. "My friends' mom said that several years ago a girl came up missing and they never found her. They said she drowned in the Kings river, but it's said she never drowned at all but that she was taken. She disappeared one day after school and was never seen or heard from again."

"And?" Constance prompted.

"And she had to pass this place every day on her way home."

Abby confirmed, "That's probably the girl you saw standing in the window, Constance."

Denise went on, "My mom says that it has something to do with this house and the old woman who lives there now."

"Have you ever seen her, Abby?"

"No, no one has."

"I would . . . I would like to see her," Constance affirmed.

"You don't know what you're saying, because it's also said that if you see her, no one will see you again," Abby warned. "Maybe she captures and keeps young girls as prisoners."

Denise volunteered and bragged, "I've seen her, you know."

Abby refuted, "No, you haven't, Denise, and no one has."

Constance reasoned, "Well, Denise, according to you, if you had seen her, you would have disappeared."

"Well, I survived," Denise defended.

"Lucky you," Constance commended.

When the three girls were down the street, some distance from the place, they noticed a car drive slowly by them and enter the gate. "That's the car I see sometimes. I wonder who it is," Denise and Abby conjectured, while Constance reflected, "I wonder where they go." The three girls continued to debate the mystery as they walked and eventually went their separate ways.

Over the years many rumors and larger-than-life stories about the old Batton manor had been weaved by children and adults alike, raised at dining room tables and before the crackling fires. As the stories were perpetuated, they evolved and seemed to grow with each telling. The tales came to include angels and demons and ghosts, hauntings, magic, and witches, caldrons and curses, and they had become part of the town's folklore and a point of keen interest and frequent debate. It was no wonder the place attracted children, both young and old who would flock to the old place, looking for a good old-fashioned scare and the chance to get a glimpse of some unnatural thing. Notwithstanding all the warnings of their parents, the children could not resist the temptation to indulge their fertile imaginations.

But as Constance eventually found out for herself, things are not always as they appear. In fact, as Constance uncovered, a Master Theodore Batton, a wealthy lord from England, purchased the land from the town and built the estate just before the turn of the century. He had become a well-respected man in the community, a friend to its people and a generous benefactor of the town. In his later years, with his health in decline, he retired to the mansion to live out his remaining years in isolation. The story goes on that Lord Batton had lived for one hundred years, up to the very day he died in the house. This had fostered many of the stories connected to the property. Now some say that old man Batton never left and that his spirit remains there still. For many years the house remained vacant, and its grounds lay in decline, unkempt and in disrepair, until one day a mysterious old woman, said to be Theodore's estranged sister, moved into the old place and renovated it, bringing it back to its former glory.

In the winter of that year, Ellen, Constance's grandmother, whom she loved dearly, died unexpectedly of complications following a bout with the flu. For many years Constance and her grandmother had been very close; beyond family, they were first and foremost best friends. The loss devastated Constance, and she fell into a period of depression.

"Constance, it's been three weeks now. It's time."

"Time for what?"

"It's time you rejoined life, don't you think?" After a single knock at the door and a moment's hesitation, Constance's mom entered her daughter's darkened room. Intent on chasing away the oppressive gloom, her mother walked straightaway over to the window and opened the drapes in order to let the light in. The rays of the sun rushed into the room, chasing away the darkness. Directing her daughter's attention to the window, she claimed, "There is life out there, Constance. Your life is out there waiting for you, and you're missing it. You'll find yourself again, I promise. You have friends who care about you."

"Grandma was my friend, Mom."

"I know."

Constance raised her frail form off the bed and raised her hand to guard her eyes from the light. Her mom sat down on the bed beside her and offered, "Abby called today."

"She did? What did she say?" Constance meekly replied.

"She wants to see you." Her mom went on, "She's worried about you too, and she's been a good and loyal friend to you for many years." Constance sat silent. Her mom continued, "You know,

Constance, no matter how much we pray or hope or dream, we can't bring her back."

"It hurts, Mom . . . so bad." She cried.

Her mom comforted, "I know, I know," as she held her close and rocked her. "It's just not possible."

"But Grandma said . . . she promised we would always be together." Constance paused and resolved, "She lied to me. I am alone now."

Her mother assured, "You are not alone. We love you and need you with us. I need you. You just have to accept it and move on with your life. I know you must be hungry." Mom suggested, "What do you say we go and get something to eat? You'll feel better." Her mother offered Constance her hand; Constance reached out and held on to her and managed an encouraging smile.

Together they went into the kitchen, where she took the first step on the path to once again regain her strength and reclaim her spirit. While Constance returned to school, to her friends and to her family, she continued to fervently and secretly pray for the return of her grandmother, believing that God would somehow someday bring her back to life; until then her tears would fill the hole left in her heart.

Every day after school Constance went to the cemetery and visited the grave of her grandmother, upon which she laid flowers, poured out her prayers, and spilled her tears. On the way to the cemetery, Constance would also stop and linger outside the iron gate of the Batton estate and look for the girl she had seen in the window some months before. Sometimes she was there, and other times the eye of the window was closed. To Constance the girl in the window was always there, ever vigilant; she thought of her, like a lamp in a lighthouse, which sent out a beacon of light into the outside world, directing wayward travelers, calling them home to her. While the massive *B* hanging on the entrance gate had been associated with the word *beware* to would-be trespassers, to Constance the meaning was simple. It stood for "Beckoned," for she was compelled by that which dwelt within.

Constance became fixated on the old house, and she obsessed about the goings-on inside. She had noticed the consistent comings and goings of what she believed to be the resident, driving a highly polished, old-model midnight-blue Packard in and out of the massive entrance gate and down the long winding driveway. Every day the gate would open, and the car would leave for some unknown rendezvous, only to return later. Constance occasionally observed an older woman dressed in a black laced dress of ancient fashion, seated in one of the large white wicker chairs on a porch, looking out into a large formal English garden. Pressed up against the wrought iron bars to one side of the gate, Constance could just make out the large formal garden. One day her vigilance was rewarded as from her vantage, she noticed what appeared to be an angel in the garden. It seemed to be glowing, emitting a radiant golden light. Constance could hardly contain her excitement at the discovery. She could not get the stunningly beautiful image out of her mind. Many times after that, she looked for the glowing angel, but just like the girl in the tower window, no one knew when she would appear. Constance was intrigued by these mysteries and was compelled to somehow discover their meaning. In order to prevent unnecessary intrusion into her affairs by her friends and family, Constance chose to keep what she was doing and what she had seen to herself; it was her secret.

Her wish was granted, as a few days later she found the entrance gate, which was normally closed, standing wide open. It was as if the place was inviting her to step inside. Setting aside her apprehension upon entering, led by curiosity, Constance cautiously walked through the gate. She fancied it a gateway to some yet undiscovered magical kingdom. Constance slowly walked up the long winding driveway, and at length she found herself in the middle of the enchanting formal English garden she had only glimpsed before. Constance was overwhelmed by the color and fragrance of the variety of flowers that adorned every corner, vase, and bed. Just as Constance bent down to smell one of the red roses, gently cradling it her hand, she was startled by a harsh voice, which called out to her from a terrace overlooking the garden.

"Just what do you think you are doing, young lady?"

Constance quickly straightened up and looked in the direction of the house. Stepping back from the flowers, Constance awkwardly answered, "I was . . . I was just going . . ."

"Going to what? Touch, or perhaps steal one of my precious roses?"

"No," Constance defended. "I just wanted to smell them."

"Huh, I know you kids. You're all the same. Admit it, you wanted to take them. You are here to destroy the beauty of this place. Well, not in here, young lady, I see you all out there," she said, pointing with a long bony finger toward the gate. "And that's why I remain in here. You just can't appreciate them where they are." The old woman stepped down off the terrace and joined Constance. The old woman continued, "But you're not even supposed to be here. How did you get in?"

"I walked in through the gate."

"That's interesting, since the gate is always closed and locked. My dear girl, an open gate is not an invitation to walk into private property."

"Really, I just . . ." Constance began again, "You have a beautiful garden. I was just admiring it, and I saw your angel glowing in the garden."

"What?"

"Your angel."

Surprised, the old woman returned, "My angel, you say . . . did she look like this?" The old woman directed Constance's attention to a stone statue standing off to one side of the garden, framed underneath a trellis.

Constance was confused and answered, "No, the angel I saw was alive, she was glowing."

The woman looked at the angel and then back at Constance questioningly. "That's impossible, child."

"I know what I saw," Constance held to her claim.

"Really, what's all this nonsense about, miss?" came the voice of a somewhat younger woman who appeared out of the house and joined the two, wiping her hands upon her apron as she walked past the old woman and straight up to Constance. She apologized to the old woman and addressed Constance sternly, ordering her to leave, threatening to call the constable. "This is private property. You are trespassing here."

"She was just leaving, Alice," the older woman assured.

"I'll show her the way out," Alice returned.

As Constance was being escorted out, on her way to the gate, she looked back and called out to the old woman, "I'm sorry for trespassing on your property," Constance said.

"I'm sure you are, and so you should be," the old woman reprimanded.

Constance added, "You have a very beautiful garden. And I really did see your angel glowing in the garden," Constance insisted.

Alice continued to press Constance in the direction she had come, directing her back through the gate, closing and latching it behind her. Constance hesitated outside the gate, looking back at the old woman. Alice reminded, "You heard the lady. Next time we'll be forced to call the authorities and have you removed."

"You believe me, don't you?" Constance pressed Alice.

"You mean about the angel?"

"It was glowing," Constance insisted.

"It's stone, it's a sculpture. By virtue of that fact, it's impossible for it to be alive . . . or glow as you say."

Constance gave up the point and fell silent. Alice dwelled for the moment, and after considering what the girl had witnessed, she continued, "You have quite an imagination, young lady, and I admire your spirit."

"But she—"

"I know," Alice assured as she looked back to the house behind her. Before leaving her company, Alice reminded, "Listen, child, I do believe you. Not everything is as it appears, and it's not always our imagination." Now it wasn't the first time Alice and her companion had heard this claim, as there was one other.

When Alice returned to the garden, Gloria asked, "Do you know who she is?"

"No, but I've seen her before standing in front of the gate."

"Doing what?"

"Just staring at the house."

Looking out toward the front gate, Gloria followed inquisitively, "Where does she go? I wonder."

"To the cemetery."

"Whatever for . . . odd girl."

"Not so odd, I think," Alice challenged.

Gloria looked strangely at Alice and ordered, "And in the future, please make sure that the gate is closed, Alice, or why not just invite the whole town in?"

"Sorry, it won't happen again."

"See that it doesn't, Alice. Wouldn't want people to get the wrong idea." The old woman stared out at Constance, who was still lingering on the wide walk in front of the mansion. Their eyes locked onto each other, and from a distance, they watched and studied each other for a time, until Constance finally turned and walked away. Alice stood alongside Gloria and, after some quiet thought, turned to her and ventured, "You think she is . . . ?"

"What?"

"The one."

"I thought we agreed not to talk about it anymore, Alice. In the future, I would appreciate it if you would keep your conjectures to yourself."

"I'm concerned about you, Gloria."

"Well, don't be," Gloria countered.

"I'm concerned about us," Alice corrected.

"One more thing, Alice," Gloria added. "Let me know if you see her again. She interests me."

"If you wish," Alice answered.

On her way into the house, something in the garden caught Alice's eye. She directed, "Gloria, look there in the garden, do you see it?"

Gloria turned to look in the direction Alice indicated. A ray of light from the sun shone down through the leaves of trees overhead and brightly illuminated the stone angel, causing it to shimmer and glow. "Almost as if it had come to life," Alice wondered aloud, and she reminded Gloria, "Jenny saw it too. Oh, how excited she was that day of her discovery. Remember, Gloria, how she is . . . how she was."

Gloria reflected for a moment. "I know . . . you didn't tell the girl, did you, Alice?"

"No, but we should have," Alice held.

Gloria directed, "Some things are just an illusion. The eyes may be tricked, and the mind can be fooled into believing in something that's not real. It's a trick of nature, no more, no less."

Alice offered, "It's a sign, Gloria, a gift of hope from God." Alice paused and thoughtfully continued, "You know, Gloria, you may be able to fool the mind, but you can't fool the heart."

Gloria finished, "She's gone, Alice . . . Jenny's gone. Just accept it."

"Maybe she's returned," Alice returned as she left her company.

That night neither Constance nor Gloria slept well, for they lay awake and reflected on their encounter earlier that day and searched the quiet darkness for the meaning of it. They didn't know that night after night they dreamed the same dream; they hoped for the same thing and pined for a miracle and an end of their grief. Each was seeking comfort from the pain of their loss. Constance wondered about the glowing angel she had seen in the garden, the girl looking out from high in the attic window. It was curious. Constance saw her grandmother in the stately old woman, and Gloria, on the other hand, could not stop thinking of how much Constance reminded her own precious granddaughter.

The next day, and every day after that, Constance would go by the house on her way to the cemetery. As she stood in front of the gate, Constance was determined to solve the mysteries that had been laid at her feet. And most of all, Constance felt that she was somehow connected to the place and the old woman who lived there, that she was part of a story that was unfolding around her.

One day, a few weeks after her encounter with the old woman, while on her way to the cemetery, the familiar blue Packard slowly pulled up in the street alongside Constance, driving next to her as she walked. The driver, whom she recognized as the younger woman referred to as Alice, who had escorted her off the property, rolled down the window and hailed, "Hello."

"Hello," Constance tritely returned, undaunted.

"My name is Alice. I never properly introduced myself to you before. It was rude of me."

"I am Constance."

"That's an unusual name," Alice noted.

"Alice is not that unusual of a name," Constance returned.

"Yes, Constance, you are right about that. Can we talk . . . please?" Alice pressed.

Constance stopped, faced Alice, and listening, waited for her to speak.

"Mrs. Vandercamp wishes the pleasure of your company. She would like you to come by the house and see her."

Constance defended, "Am I in trouble?"

"No, not at all, it's not about that."

"Why does she want to see me then?"

"That's a fair question. She wants to meet you and get to know you. Apparently she wants to make amends for your awkward encounter the last time."

"But I thought you—"

Alice interrupted, "It's your choice of course, Constance, and given the way things were left the last time you met, I'm sure she'll understand if you don't. She would be disappointed of course, but it's important to keep in mind that she has opened her house to you, and for her that is something. She has asked me to speak on her behalf, believing that you may not want to talk to her. She would like me to tell you that she would appreciate it if you would accept her apology and would like the opportunity to formally introduce herself to you as the nice, pleasant elderly lady she is and not the old cantankerous spinster she presented when last you met. She is concerned that she left the wrong impression and means to correct it personally. She would like for you to come to the house tomorrow afternoon between three and three thirty p.m., if you are able. What can I tell her?"

Constance heard a muffled noise come from deep in the back seat of the car, as if someone were trying to clear their throat. Constance strained to see beyond the driver and turned her attention to the rear passenger window that was blacked out. She looked back at the driver again and affirmed, trading her trepidation in for interest in the meeting, "Please tell her yes, I would like to meet her."

"That will make the old woman happy. I will let her know your answer." As Alice placed the car in gear, preparing to go, she abruptly applied the brake, hesitated momentarily, and added an afterthought, "You know," she paused, "it's been a very long time since we—" she stopped short and corrected, "since she has entertained anyone at the house. I will open the gate for you. Until tomorrow then?"

"I get out of school at three o'clock," Constance added.

"We know," Alice claimed matter-of-factly.

"See you then," Constance answered, and she wondered, curious how she knew that.

*　　*　　*

"The following day, Constance arrived at the old place. She entered the wide gate, but this time as a formally invited guest."

"But, Grandma, weren't you, I mean, wasn't Constance scared?" Raven interrupted.

"No, little one," her grandma explained. "To Constance the place wasn't scary at all, as her friends had led her to believe. To Constance, it was an opportunity to unravel the mysteries that surrounded the house and the old woman that lived there, a chance to live in a story of which she was already a part." Constance continued to read.

*　　*　　*

Now as Constance entered the gate and walked along the long winding driveway, she was reminded of the famous children's stories of *Alice In Wonderland* and *The Wizard Of Oz*. She fancied it an entrance to her wonderland, and the driveway a grand avenue, her very own yellow brick road, which would lead her to a magical castle. Upon arrival at the house, Constance felt very small next to the massive structure; she hadn't remembered it being that big. She continued to follow the path around the house, which led to the garden, and found the old woman sitting under the shade of a tree in the garden, anxiously awaiting her arrival.

"Over here, child," she beckoned.

Constance came to stand next to her. A somewhat rigid and reserved silence gripped the moment. Constance broke the silence with, "I'm really sorry about the last time."

The old woman promptly returned, "No, dear, you didn't do anything wrong. It was me, and I want to apologize for the way I treated you. I hope you can find it in your heart to forgive me, and that we can be friends. I am the Mrs. Vandercamp, that mean old witch that Alice and, I suspect, your friends have told you about. But my friends call me Gloria. It would please me if you would call me Gloria."

"If you call me Constance."

"It's a deal." Gloria offered her hand, and they shook on it, smiling at each other as they shook hands. "And don't tell those friends of yours any different, wouldn't want them to get the idea that I was really a nice old lady."

"Agreed." They laughed at the thought. Gloria went on, "I'm not good with people, please forgive me. I don't have many visitors."

Constance returned, "I'm not good with people either. My friends think that I'm weird or something. I have to wonder what they're saying now." They both laughed, as the ice between the two continued to thaw. She offered Constance a chair next to her and motioned, "Please sit down with me here in the garden." She next held out to Constance a single-long stem crimson rose, which she had cut from her garden. "Here, I wanted you to have this. Think of it as sort of a peace offering."

Constance was taken with the old woman's charm and graciously accepted. "Thank you." Noticing a book in the old woman's lap, Constance asked, "What's that book you're reading?"

"Oh, it's my story that I've been writing."

"How interesting," Constance mused.

"It's not finished," Gloria added.

Constance noticed the glasses around her neck and offered, "Would you like me to read it back to you?"

"No, it's not necessary. Why don't we just sit here and talk and get to know each other for starters? People are so much more interesting in person than in a book, don't you think so?" She carefully laid the book aside and asked Constance, "Do you like to read, dear?"

"I love to read. I'm surrounded by books at home. One of these days I'll bring my favorite book and read it to you if you like," Constance suggested.

"I would like that, very much. My eyes are tired, and I can't see to read that well anymore. Of course you've met Alice. She normally reads to me here in the garden. It's one of the few pleasures afforded an old woman considerably lessened by the loss of one most precious child."

"I'm sorry," Constance followed.

Not wanting to continue to dwell on it, Gloria quickly went on, "I have a large library inside the house, full of books I have collected over the years. Perhaps you would like to see it sometime."

Constance' eyes sparkled, and she said, "Oh yes, I can imagine what it must be like, to have so many books, to be able to go so many places."

After that day, their differences quickly drifted off into the past, and at the behest of her host, Constance visited many, many more times over the next several months. There was something fulfilling that Constance found in Gloria's presence, and Gloria found her life enriched by knowing Constance. And so their friendship flourished as they shared themselves with each other.

Constance and Gloria traveled many places in the arms of each other's company. They spent countless hours together in the garden, tending the flowers while they talked about their past, their future, their dreams and adventures, and seemingly covering everything else under the sun in their longwinded conversations. They even tried their hand at baking; unfortunately, it didn't turn out so well, and at the request of Alice, who was both an excellent cook and domestically inclined, the two were required to confine their activities to everywhere else but the kitchen.

*　　*　　*

"Did they bake cookies, Grandma?" Raven asked.

"They tried to make cookies, little one, but unfortunately, they burned the cookies and made a mess."

"Were they sad because they got in trouble, Grandma?"

"Not really, dear," Constance explained.

*　　*　　*

Gloria and Constance didn't mind being dismissed from the kitchen; as a matter of fact, they were happy with the arrangement as Alice insisted on serving the two refreshments in the garden. Constance related to Gloria, "You know, I could get used to this." To which Gloria replied, "I already have, dear, for some years now." And they laughed.

As Constance and Gloria continued to reveal themselves to each other, taking Constance's hand in hers, Gloria admitted, "Constance . . . I've been meaning to tell you for some time now. Do you remember when you told me about the glowing angel in my garden?"

"Yes, I remember. How could I forget something like that?"

"You never asked about it after that, why not?" Gloria queried.

"I don't know . . . I guess, it really isn't important anymore. I mean, we have each other, right?"

"You are so sweet, Constance. Yes, we have each other. I just wanted you to know that you were right all along . . . about the angel in my garden."

Constance leaned forward and excitedly squeezed Gloria's hand. "You saw it?"

"Yes, I've seen it. Oh, my dear girl, sometimes what we are searching for is right there in front of our eyes. In order to see things, we have to open our hearts and minds and believe."

"It's your angel," Constance corrected.

"My angel," Gloria capitulated.

"I told you she was there. I'm so happy," Constance celebrated.

"Me too, child, me too." Gloria continued, "You are not the first to see her. Someone else . . ." Gloria thought of her own grand-daughter and stopped short of saying her name, "very dear to me saw the glowing angel too, a long time ago."

Now to say that the old woman looked forward to Constance's visits would be an understatement. They had become inseparable. Seeking assurance from Constance, Gloria inquired on more than one occasion, "Now you know you're going to come and see me tomorrow again. Please do, won't you? Now I'm not going anywhere. I'll be right here anxiously awaiting your return."

Constance, who was excited about their visits as well, inno-cently teased, "You know I always come to see you, *But* . . . I'm not sure I can tomorrow." Oh, how Gloria hated the *but* word.

*   *   *

Raven interrupted, "Grandma, I know it's not like my butt or something, but," Raven giggled at her use of the word, "why didn't the woman like the word *but?*"

"Because when you say it, it means that there are strings attached to a promise. Like if I told you that I would take you to get ice cream, *but* you would have to be good. Understand?"

"Yeah, I understand. If the woman was good, then Constance would come to see her."

"Yes, Raven, something like that. Anyway, where was I? Oh yes."

*   *   *

Now Constance could not bear to see Gloria sad or disap-pointed, and she therefore quickly recanted, "Of course I'll come by tomorrow." Like a giddy schoolgirl, the joy returned to Gloria's face, and this made Constance very happy.

Concerned about the amount of time Constance was spending with her, Gloria asked, "You're not going to get into trouble from your mother for spending so much time with this old woman, are you? Now be honest."

"No, not at all, my mom wants me to make new friends." Constance further thought out loud, "Of course, it might help if you were to write me a note."

The two laughed jovially at the thought, and Gloria admitted, "Oh, my dear, sweet child, you are a delight to my soul. Since we're on the subject, there is one more small thing you could do for me, Constance."

"Anything, just name it," Constance opened.

"Would you, by chance, call me Grandma? It would make a certain old woman very happy."

Constance fell silent and looked at Gloria lovingly for a moment.

Gloria added, "Of course you don't have to. I was just thinking that—"

"Of course I'll call you Grandma if you like. I would be happy to do it."

Gloria reached out to Constance and spoke, "Come here, child." They hugged each other tightly, and upon leaving Gloria that day, Constance confirmed, "I'll see you tomorrow. I love you, Grandma."

Constance spent less time now visiting the grave of her grandmother as her continuing, frequent visits with Gloria were so delightful and had become the highlight of her life. And so they shared each other's company daily, with exception of a few unavoidable conflicts.

And there were things that the two did not share openly, for each carried the pain of their loss alone, and for a time they would hold their grief hostage. They continued to keep this conversation at a distance, for it was an emotional bridge that neither was willing to cross; but the truth, which cannot be denied, will come out sooner or later. Constance noticed that at times Gloria was distracted and would stare off into the distance beyond her, entertaining some melancholy thought. The sorrow etched on the old woman's face, which was made old and weary by life and loss, was apparent. Constance realized that referring to Gloria as Grandma seemed to lift her spirits and served to reinforce the close bond that was building between them.

From the window that looked out into the garden, Alice watched the two grow closer, and she was exceedingly glad about it;

she saw Gloria come back to life, and like the garden, their friendship blossomed into so much more.

And the day of truth came to visit them. Constance arrived somewhat later than usual. She found Gloria seated on the porch, looking out toward the gate, anxiously awaiting her arrival. "Sorry I'm late," Constance called out as she ascended the steps.

"You have nothing to be sorry about, dear girl. I was just reading this book . . . or trying to read this book. Please sit down, dear. Would you like some tea and cakes? I just made them myself this afternoon."

Alice, standing just inside the house, challenged, "Made them, did you, Gloria? Hello, Constance."

"Hi, Alice," Constance acknowledged.

Gloria recognized, "Oh, Alice, didn't know you were there, have to change my story now."

"I'll leave you two to tell your stories then. Of course in your case, Gloria, I think tall tales would be the operative word," Alice followed, and they all enjoyed a laugh about it.

"I'm so glad you're here," Gloria spoke as she took Constance's hand and guided her to the chair beside her. "And what is this?" Gloria directed as she leaned forward to inspect the book that Constance had conspicuously laid on the table before her.

Constance explained, "Do you remember when I said I would bring my favorite book over and read it to you? Well . . . this is my favorite book. It's *The Wooden Angel* by William Frances Ramkan."

Gloria sat back deep in the chair with a look of astonishment.

Constance asked, "Do you know this book, Grandma?"

"Know it . . . oh yes, I know it well."

As Gloria's eyes began to well up with heavy tears, Constance, concerned, asked, "Are you all right, Gloria?"

Gloria answered, her voice quivering, "It is a very sad book."

"Yes, but it has a happy ending," Constance reminded. "Didn't you like the book?"

"I love the book, and it was her favorite as well . . ."

Not sure what to say, Constance sat silent, holding Gloria's hand.

Gloria composed herself, laid her hand on the book, and continued, "Sometimes, Constance, I see you look at the upper attic window. It's like you've seen a ghost or something. What is it, child? Please tell me what you see."

Constance's thoughts raced. It was a mystery yet undiscovered. It was something the two friends never spoke of, Constance not wanting to ask and Gloria not willing to tell. Like the angel in the garden that Gloria had initially denied, she seemed ready to reveal the secret of the girl in the window.

Constance began, "I don't . . . I don't know, but it looks like there's a girl standing in the attic window. Sometimes I would see her from the street, but I haven't seen her for a long time." Constance continued, "She looked lonely, like she was watching, or waiting for something."

Alice, who was standing close by, interjected, "Maybe for you, Constance."

"For me! How could that be though?"

Privately, Alice had encouraged Gloria to let Constance into her life—to open the drapes that shaded her heart. Neither Gloria nor Alice was willing to talk about it, because there was no going back; it was time. Alice pressed Gloria in front of Constance, "Are you sure you want to do this now? There is no going back."

Gloria committed, "Maybe it's time we stop hiding behind our denial and tell her the truth, about everything." Gloria rose out of her chair, took Constance by the hand, and gently spoke, "Come with me, child, I want to show you something."

Until then, Constance had been in every room in the house save one, the attic. Gloria had kept her house like she had kept her heart, sealed and closed to all, but this girl had become so much more. Gloria finally decided to let Constance all the way into her life.

Followed by Alice, hand in hand Gloria and Constance ascended the grand staircase, through one door, and then through another. Up and up until at last they reached one final door. Beyond the door, a loft occupied the small space in the uppermost part of the mansion. It was a dimly lit room, more like a small secret chamber, Constance reflected. Inside the room there was a bed, a chair, a dresser, a chest, and a lamp, which always burned and bathed the room in a perpetual soft light. Gloria stepped over to the drawn curtains and opened them. Light quickly flooded the small tidy room. There she stood.

"This is," Gloria introduced the form standing by the window, "what you saw."

"Yes."

"It is a dress form, dear."

"What?"

"A manikin."

Constance realized that since she had started to come to visit Gloria, the drapes had been drawn and closed to the room. Constance just stood in wonder, staring at the form, and wondered about its significance.

Gloria continued, "It was another phase of my life, and it doesn't matter now. The form wears a dress I was making for my granddaughter. I never finished it." Gloria looked around the space and reflected, "It's been a long time since I have been in this room, Constance."

Constance pored over the few things carefully placed on the table. Among them was the book *The Wooden Angel*. She noticed the book. Surprised, she looked back at Gloria. Gloria confirmed, "That was her favorite book too." The closeness that the two had shared began to come to light and finally make sense, that indeed they might have more in common than she once thought. Constance looked closely at the other items and picked up a hair brush off the dresser. Gloria realized that she could not bear her granddaughter's things to be touched and immediately admonished Constance, "No! Don't touch anything." She retrieved the brush from Constance.

"I'm sorry, I didn't know."

Gloria directed, "I want you to go now."

"But . . ." Constance stammered.

"Please, Constance, just leave me alone now. I thought I was ready. I was wrong to bring you up here now, like this."

Alice, who was standing just outside the door, quickly came into the room and asked, "Is everything all right?"

"Please take the child out of here. She was just leaving," Gloria demanded.

Constance remembered these very words spoken to her at the time of their first meeting in the garden. "Yes, of course, I will. You sure you're okay, Gloria?"

"I'm fine." Gloria sat down in the chair in front of the desk and looked blankly into the small vanity mirror.

Alice coaxed, "Come on, child, there's nothing more we can do here."

Constance was confused. Upon leaving, she looked back at Gloria seated in the chair, clutching the brush and quietly weeping, repeating, "My Jenny, my poor Jenny." Constance felt her pain. "I really am sorry, child," Gloria called to Constance as she left her company. Referencing the pain of the loss she felt at the death of her granddaughter, Gloria finished, "Please understand, child. I just can't put myself through that again." Now to see her friend, of whom she had grown so fond, like this broke Constance's heart.

Upon exiting the house, Alice stopped Constance on the porch and directed her to sit down with her. She took Constance's hands in hers and confided all. "You know it's not your fault, Constance. You could not have known." After a pause, Alice directed, "She never told you, did she?"

"Told me what?" Constance trembled, on the brink of tears.

"A year ago she lost her only granddaughter. That's where I take her every day, to the cemetery to visit Jenny's grave. She lived with us in this house. They were very close, as you can imagine. She lived in that room of the house up until the day she died, those were her things. This was a happy place then." Alice reflected and continued, "The happiness was finally returning when you came into her life, you dear girl. I had warned her it might be too soon. She rightly protested. I see now that I was wrong about you. I just didn't want her to be hurt again, and grief is now the result of her indulgence in hope. It broke our hearts when it happened."

"I didn't know." Constance broke down and cried, as she repeated over and over, "I didn't know, I didn't know."

Alice reached out to her, pulled her into her close, and comforted, "Poor girl, poor, poor girl. You're the best thing that's come into her life since then. You need to know that. There, there, it's not your fault. She'll come around, you'll see. She can't live without you now." Alice was gentle and understanding. "She loves you, you know, like her own precious granddaughter. You remind her so much of her Jenny. Something else you don't know . . . Gloria is my sister. I came to live with her to help her through the grief, but no one can replace a granddaughter—or a grandmother."

"You knew," Constance looked up at Alice with tears streaming down her face.

Alice dried Constance's eyes with her hankie, as she confirmed, "Yes, Constance, I knew. That's where you go, isn't it?"

"Sometimes," Constance replied.

"You know her heart is set on you. She needs you just as much as you need her." Constance looked at Alice with wet eyes, and Alice continued, "I can see you're hurting too, and your loss is also apparent." Alice paused and proposed, "Constance, tomorrow morning, I will be taking Gloria to the cemetery again, where she will lay flowers on the grave of her granddaughter. Listen, and this is really important, I want you to also be there at the cemetery in the morning when we arrive."

"But . . . she won't want to see me, Alice," Constance questioned.

Alice directed, "Trust me, she will want to see you. Promise me, dear, do this for Gloria, for me . . . for you We will make things right," Alice promised, and she confirmed, "Until then, okay, Constance?"

"Okay," Constance sniffled.

Alice added, "No matter what happened here today, trust your heart, Constance. Believe in what you know is the truth, that you deserve love from each other. Don't give up on her. She needs you— and so do I. When you came into our lives, it is as though the sun had returned. Tomorrow you will both find peace and a new beginning. Your friendship will stand. Everything will be all right, you'll see." Alice watched Constance slowly walk away, before looking back briefly. Alice encouraged and repeated, "It's okay, dear, everything will be all right, you'll see." With that, Constance turned and walked away, and Alice went back into the house.

Later that evening, Alice and Gloria had a long talk about things that mattered. Seated opposite each other in the drawing room, after a long silence, Gloria began, "You told her then?"

"Of course. I told her everything," Alice confirmed and continued to instruct, "You need her as much she needs you, and I need her too. It wasn't right keeping the truth from her. You know that as well as me. It's time we let a little joy and happiness in here, and that's the girl who brought it to us. If you let her go, you will regret it forever. God sent her to us, Gloria."

Gloria then reminded Alice, "God took Jenny away from me."

"We will have to live with the decisions we make and attempt to survive the consequences of our actions."

Gloria resigned, "It's too late. What have I done?"

Alice consoled, "What are you talking about? It's not too late, yet. There is, however, a point of no return. It will be too late when you're dead."

Gloria added, "She hates me now."

Alice assured, "She doesn't hate you, she loves you. She was scared and confused and didn't understand because we didn't tell her, Gloria. Despite what you think, the truth won't drive her away. It will bring her back to us."

"What have we done?" Gloria wept.

Alice convicted, "We've made a mess of things and broke that little girl's heart is what we've done. We need to fix things now, and if you won't, I will."

"Yes, Alice, you're right, just tell me what to do," Gloria resigned.

It was a long walk to the gate; Constance felt cold and alone again, and she pined for her own grandmother. As she reached the end of the long drive, she turned to look back and up to the attic window. The drapes were once again closed. Constance remembered Alice's words from earlier: "There is a reason Gloria closed those drapes and closed the room. It's because you have returned, so she extinguished the light, which incessantly searched the darkness for life, for love, for light, for you. She finally started to believe that miracles could indeed happen, that something wonderful could arise out of tragedy. Constance, you are her miracle."

Constance arrived at the cemetery early the next morning. She knelt on the grave of her grandmother where she lay under a soft mound of earth covered with lush green grass. With her finger, Constance traced the words she had specially engraved into the stone. It read simply, "To Ellen, my grandma, I love you always—Constance." She backed away and sat on a stone bench.

*   *   *

"On this bench, Grandma?" Raven asked.

"Yes, dear, it was this very bench, amidst the flowers and lush grass."

*   *   *

Constance waited. A short time later, the now-familiar blue Packard quietly drove up. She watched as Gloria and Alice got out of the car, and arm in arm they walked the short distance to the grave of Gloria's granddaughter, where they stopped and stood reverently. Gloria raised her eyes and saw Constance. Constance stood up and walked over to the foot of her grandmother's grave site, facing Gloria.

Breaking the silence, Gloria asked, "What are you doing here, child?" Gloria's heart dropped as she realized the answer to her question was before her. She walked around to the headstone opposite her granddaughter's, and now standing next to Constance, she read the inscription aloud, "In memory of Ellen Elders, 1890–1990." Gloria stopped reading when she got to Constance's name inscribed at the bottom of the stone and looked back at Constance, astonished. She trembled at the thought as she spoke, "This is . . ." Gloria stopped.

"My grandmother," Constance confirmed and continued, "Grandma, this is Gloria, the one I told you about. She is my best friend in the whole world."

Gloria immediately reached out and swept Constance up in her arms. She openly thanked God; there Gloria's beloved granddaughter and Constance's grandmother rest together in the ground, head to head.

And then, came that one, singular moment where there are no words, but the absolute astonishment, the instant recognition, shared only by those who witness something they can't explain or comprehend. They realize they are all a part of a profound miracle, the contradiction to all we temporally know or think we know. We are overwhelmed and swept away by it.

Constance, Gloria, and Alice realized their prayers had been answered on that Christmas morning, and everything they went through had led up to this one impactful moment, which all began with one not-so-chance encounter not two years earlier. And together, arm in arm they walked back to the car, leaving the life they had planned behind them in order to have the life that was waiting for them.

*   *   *

"And let's not forget the most important thing of all, Raven."

"What's the most important thing, Grandma?"

Constance placed the tip of her finger playfully on Raven's nose and answered with a big smile, "And they lived happily ever after . . ."

Raven smiled back at Constance and said, "I like happy endings, Grandma."

"So do I," Constance agreed.

When Constance was finished reading the book to Raven, she claimed, "And that's the end, until it begins again." She set the book in her lap, looked down at Raven, and asked, "Did you like the story?"

Raven answered right away, "I liked the book very much, Grandma," but Raven looked puzzled and added, "I have one question."

"Yes, dear, what is it?"

"Why are there a lot of blank pages left in the book?"

Constance commended, "That's a very good question, Raven." Constance picked up the book and carefully placed it in Raven's little hands, adding, "My story is finished. The blank pages are for you to write your story on."

"Really, you mean this is my book now?"

"It is yours now, my gift to you."

"Oh, thank you, Grandma. I love it, thank you. I love you so much. Do you believe that fairy tales can come true, Grandma, just like the *Wizard of Oz* and *Alice in Wonderland*?"

"Hey there, I thought you only had one question, little one."

"I did have one question, but now I have another question."

"It's okay, that's what children do best, you know."

"What do they do, Grandma?"

"They ask questions, lots and lots of questions."

"Oh," Raven giggled and followed up with, "Are there really ghosts and witches too, Grandma?"

Constance offered simply, "I don't know about fairy tales or ghosts or witches, dear, but I can tell you what I do know—I believe in the magic of Christmas. I believe that God answers the prayers of people that believe, that angels are real, and that miracles happen, and you, Raven, are a living proof of that."

"What do you mean, Grandma?"

"You are one of my most precious miracles."

"I am, Grandma?"

"You most certainly are."

Raven looked at the grave of her grandma's friend, Gloria, which was now next to Constance's grandmother, and wondered, "Grandma, do you really think that Gloria was actually grandma Ellen too?"

"Yes, about that . . . you know, Raven, in the book, when Constance said that her grandma left her all alone when she died, even though she said she would always be with her?"

"Yes, I remember."

"Well, people don't die. They live on in the hearts, minds, and spirits of others, so when I tell you that I will be with you always, believe that I will. You may not recognize my face, but you will know my spirit."

"But how will I know if it's really you, Grandma?"

"You will know me and feel me in here." Constance put her hand on Raven's chest, right over her heart.

"You mean in my heart."

"Yes, Raven, in your heart."

"Oh, I see, that will be like a new house where you will live."

"Yes, it will be my new house."

"I like that, Grandma."

"Me too, dear, me too."

As the two sat quietly together in the fading light of day, not quite satisfied, Raven asked one more question. "Grandma, what happened to the girl in the window?"

"It wasn't a girl after all. She was like a lighthouse, which shines its light out in the darkness and leads people home when they are lost. This light was meant for Constance."

"Who was shining the light, Grandma?"

"God was shining the light, little one."

"Did anyone else see the light, or just Constance?"

"Oh, I think others saw the light too, but they weren't drawn to the light like she was." Constance looked at the little girl next to her and said thoughtfully, "I had to see who was shining the light."

"You were the girl in the story, Grandma?"

"Yes, Raven, it was me."

"I just knew it, Grandma, because I would go see who was the shining the light too."

"I know, little one, because you're just like me, Raven. You have to see it for yourself."

(by Darrell W. McNabb, 2014)

The Woman Who Talked to Animals

That was his love. She talked to the birds, and they talked to her. She understood them, and as his love reminded, "the good done to them always comes back to you."

He was there in the beginning, when his lady was both young and beautiful, when they were new creatures and the splendor of springtime adorned the garden of their lives. It was that time before the winter set upon their love and undid them, that time before his lady fell out of the nest and broke her wing. And he was also there when, in her later years, ugliness betrayed her beauty, for what happened to her could not be described in gentler terms. It was the frailty of old age and debilitating disease that had twisted and contorted her body and held her hostage to the end. And not unlike a thief, it snatched away from her that grace, which the creator had so generously bestowed upon her in her youth. Yet she, who forever remained beautiful to him, was both the inspiration and benefactor of this beautiful story, which I now relate.

As he was a reflective soul, preferring his own company to that of others, the old man searched out solace from the fast-paced world in odd and sundry places, like the cemetery, the church, or the library where he found seclusion, solitude, and serenity. And when it suited him, he engaged in relating to or rather watching his fellow human beings in a more animated setting, like the mall, the bowling alley, or the Laundromat, where he found himself once again. It was his singularly familiar respite from the madness of the chaotic world beyond, and most importantly his connection to people, to life. He fancied himself a passenger on a fast-moving train; while he remained motionless, he viewed the world rushing by him through the windows, frame by frame. As it was winter, again the old man's bones were appreciative of the numerous washing machines and driers that heated the place to a tolerable temperature.

He sat quietly in a remote part of the interior, taking it all in, when an ancient relic of a woman, hunched over, deformed with severe lordosis, and clothed in what appeared to be no more than layered rags, entered there. With keen interest he watched the old woman waddle into the Laundromat, carrying a mere two old tattered gray woolen stockings in her hands. She put one stocking in a washing machine, while the other, which seemed to contain something, she folded and stuffed deeply into the right front pocket of her overcoat. She next walked over to one of the heavy metal chairs and, for a time, just stood and stared at it. After contemplating the chair, she walked over to the door and propped it open with a rock. She returned to the chair and grasped it firmly with both hands, and with some difficulty and while making one hell of a racket, she slowly dragged it out the door. After placing the chair against the glass front, she reached into her pocket and pulled out the stocking, carefully opened it up, and methodically sprinkled its contents—bread crumbs, nuts, and seeds—out onto the cracked and weathered concrete walk in front of the Laundromat. Satisfied, she turned, placed her wide rump in position, and backed into the chair. Balancing her bulky frame with her hands, she slowly lowered her quivering body down into it. Upon nearing the bottom, she collapsed the rest of the way. She folded her hands and placed them in her lap and exhaled heavily from her labors. With the stage now set, the old woman quietly waited, looking out and up, mumbling incoherently. What exactly was her plan, one could only guess. She now had the attention of everyone there, and she waited there in the midst of the mutterings of onlookers. "What's she doing out there?" echoed from the gallery as the patrons fell over each other to get a better look at this curious, quirky old woman.

A gentleman sitting next to the man had since set down the paper he was pretending to read and focused on the old woman as well; he ridiculed, "Crazy old woman, takes all kinds, that's for sure." He nudged the old man and continued to make sport of the old woman, "Looks like she thinks she's going feed some squirrels, birds, or something."

"Or something," the old man agreed.

"I've been coming here a long time, and I never seen squirrels, let alone birds—unless she can make them magically appear out of thin air."

The old man turned to him and observed, "Not very trusting, are you? You ever heard of Cinderella, Mary Poppins, or Dr. Doolittle?"

"What! What's that got to do with anything?"

The man looked back at the woman and reflected, "Maybe nothing, maybe everything."

"You're as crazy as she is."

He ignored the man's intrusion into his space and dismissed his cynicism, for sadly, he had forgotten how to dream. The man recalled a time when his own skepticism clouded his mind, preventing him from seeing beyond only what his eyes permitted him to see. He all along knew what was about to happen there at the Laundromat had indeed happened before.

And so he sat back deep into his chair, turned off the moment, and went back to that day long ago in his life. He saw and understood this familiar old woman and remembered how his beloved wife loved to sing and to whistle, using her angelic voice to call the birds from their nests and perches to join her in her garden where she cared for each and every one of them. And right on cue came the birds; dozens of them descended from the sky, upon the wind, and appeared before her where they sat perched on her head, arms, and legs. And she stroked them and fed them and knew each one by name.

Amazed at this, he recalled asking her, "How do you do it?"

"Do what?" She played.

"You know what I mean. How do they know? First, they are nowhere around, and then poof, they are everywhere—like magic."

She smiled, and in her soft and gentle voice, she said, "Yes, dear, I know what you mean. They know me, and when I call them, they come to me, where they are safe. Here, they can eat their fill and rest from their labors. They are mine and I am theirs."

"Maybe it's telepathy or something," he reasoned.

"Or magic . . . or nature." She smiled.

He ultimately concluded that she had an extraordinary gift. There was no other explanation for it. He was reminded of that famous Franciscan friar, Saint Francis of Assisi, the patron saint of animals, known for his love for all of God's creatures and the care he provided those animals that happened on his path, and the stories of how he could talk to the animals and understand them. That was his love. She talked to the birds, and they talked to her. She understood them.

Ever since he had known her, she had been the target of birds, as they baptized her from above. Out of everyone in her company, the birds always seemed to find her. And it didn't just happen some-times, in some places; it happened all the time and everywhere she went. One may consider it unlucky if a bird poops on your head; she thought of it more as an anointing, like she was marked, per-haps chosen for some higher purpose. And they all laughed, probably because they weren't the ones whom the birds pooped on. While he had teased her about it early on, he also began to think that just maybe there was something more to it.

The beginning of their story is not unlike so many others. Following their dreams as childhood sweethearts, the couple even-tually married and began their adult lives in an otherwise unremark-able house located at the end of secluded drive, at the edge of small mountain town. In the middle of the front yard, there grew a very big and very old weeping willow tree, which eclipsed the small house and was a prominent landmark on the street, demanding long looks from passersby. When they first arrived at their new home years earlier, the two lovers etched their initials upon its trunk, leaving their perma-nent mark upon the very place they began their lives together; and as the tree grew, so did their initials. They raised a family, two boys, assorted pets (dogs particularly), and a beautiful, expansive garden. Early on the family established the tradition that every Christmas they would decorate and illuminate the willow tree with hundreds of lights, and every year the decorations became more elaborate than the year before. It didn't take long before the decorated tree caught the interest of the town, and people came from all over to view its splendor and bathe in its light. It was an inspiring sight indeed. Now when it came to decorating the old willow, above all else, Will's wife, Jane, was insistent that God would be able to see it from heaven, and so their work was certainly cut out for them; the blessing it brought to their family and the community was apparent. As she got older, even though she was unable to help decorate the tree herself, she insisted on overseeing every detail of the decorations. The family also adopted another tradition, as on those cold winter nights of Christmas, they would sit together on the porch, bundled up in a warm blanket made by the hands of generations past. And settled in with their hot chocolate and other seasonal spirits, together they would toast Christmas, enjoy the beautiful tree, and sing the Christmas carols of old.

Years were but days, and her beloved boys grew up, moved away, and had families of their own. For some years the grandchildren visited, and she shared with them her love of gardening, the secret of talking to the birds and animals, and to respect the beauty of nature. And as was their tradition, the family continued to come together at Christmas, decorate the willow tree, share each other's company, and reminisce about old times. The grandchildren were always happy to update the old folks on the new world, which was fast leaving them behind, and the old folks caught the grandchildren up on what they had missed during their fast-moving ride through life. But at Christmas, for one brief night they would come together and freeze time.

There came a time when the grandchildren no longer visited, as they grew up and went their way and attended traditions of their own. And it was as it was in the beginning; the two young lovers, now old, were alone together once more. While they pined for the company of their extended family and to fill the void left by their absence, she, along with her husband, immersed herself in tending to her lavish garden and charged herself with caring for God's many creatures, both great and small, who came and went there to escape the chaos of an ever-changing, unpredictable world. In her domain time seemed to stand still, and they were safe in this realm of balance and order. Over the years he helped her till and plant and feed the many trees, shrubs, and flowers and create winding cobblestone walks leading the fortunate soul to some secret reflection pond, fountains attended by stately statuary, and gazebos framed in lavish hedges. And most importantly, the addition of many miniature houses, and feeding stations for her beloved birds. "Build it and they will come," she reminded. Over time the two had created an elaborate garden in which one could literally lose themselves. It was indeed a labyrinth of beauty and of serenity, and it was a heavenly world in which she was quite content to live out the rest of her days.

The garden was an enchanted place for both beauty and beast alike. It was a special place of respite for the many creatures she protected and watched over, and she was the guardian of the garden. It was in this special place where the flowers and flying things reigned, a place where flora and fauna flourished in the magic of her presence. All manner of things were welcome, from the squirrel, to the cat, the dog, the birds, and the bees; from the spider to the butterfly, the snail, and the snake; all things that flew, slithered, sulked, and crawled. Just as he was the chronicler of the events of their time, she was the author of it, and they were all a part of her creation.

At the center of this enchanted realm, out of all her subjects, her beloved birds she favored, followed by her loyal dogs. "I think you like birds most, and your dogs of course, and me at times, I think."

"Oh, so you think that's the way it is, huh?"

"Just an observation."

"I love you and my birds and my dogs."

"In that order?" he queried.

"There is no order for those who live within the realm of my heart, dear."

Relieved, he went on about her fascination with birds. "All the other creatures fend for themselves, but you go out of your way to feed the birds. I mean, I get it, dogs are totally dependent on us, but birds, they have the world. They fly anywhere, and you feed them a buffet in your backyard. They are freeloaders."

"Well, you are partly right, they are free. You don't understand. You don't know birds like I do."

"I know they need to get a job!" he pointed out and went on to explain, "If you feed the birds, what have you got? Fat birds, that's what."

"You are so cynical, dear. This is their job, don't you know?"

"I'm joking of course," he resigned, "as long as it makes you happy, dear."

She smiled and answered simply, "Yes, it makes me very happy."

He added, "When I die, I want to come back as a bird, or dog, just to be with you."

She smiled. Even though birds fought for her favor, she loved them all notwithstanding, and she liked them for different reasons.

"I love my life here in the garden with you and with all my friends," she reinforced, for over the years, she had gradually cut herself off from people, choosing to remain focused on her delightful garden and her bird friends. After being thwarted by fair-weather friends in the past, she claimed, "I prefer fair-feathered friends as opposed to fair-weather friends. They are loyal and devoted, and their love is uncomplicated and unconditional." Of course it made perfect sense. She reminded, "You know that the birds talk to me?"

The man shrugged his shoulders.

"Well, they do," she insisted. She whistled softly, and as if on cue, a group of hummingbirds swooped down and surrounded her, and two in particular, a female she named Persnickety and a male that she named Dart, came to rest upon the end of her finger and remarkably allowed her to kiss each of them on the top of their heads. Will looked on in amazement. He recalled that more than once he faced rejection when he had tried to touch one of these illusive creatures, and he also remembered that more than once Jane had introduced the concepts of patience and gentleness to him, which continued to fly over his head.

"Show off," he charged her, and wondered, "Why did you give her that name, and how do you know it's a girl? Did you lift up the tail feathers and check?"

She laughed at the thought and said, "No, you silly boy. First, Persnickety here, she can be obstinate and quite possessive of the feeder, can't you, little one?" The little bird just tilted its tiny head to one side, looked at the man, stuck out its tongue, as if to punctuate her keeper's remark, and flew off, followed by the other, which shot off like a dart. "And that's how Dart got his name," she pointed out.

"I see what you mean," he acknowledged.

And she continued, "The difference between the two is that the males are very brightly colored, and the females are dull so they can better blend into the natural surroundings and avoid predators."

"Girls are more cunning," he offered.

"I prefer cautious, and they live longer too."

"Boys are targets."

"Protectors," she corrected.

"Protectors," he agreed.

"Along with dragonflies, they are my garden fairies. They're like fairies, don't you think?"

"And you're the fairy godmother," he returned. They laughed and enjoyed their time together.

The old man recalled his granddaughter asking if Grandma was magic. When he asked her why, she thought that she said, "Because she can talk to animals, like me."

Grandfather prompted, "Now I wonder who taught you to do that."

"Grandma," she charged.

And grandfather went on to tell her some extraordinary stories about her grandma. "Let me tell you about your grandma," he began. "Now I don't know if your grandma is magic or not, but I have seen her do some amazing, remarkable things." And they settled into the backyard swing, and he opened, "I have seen your grandma bring a dead hummingbird back to life. It was cold that winter, so cold in fact that birds would freeze instantly and fall from the sky if they tried to fly." Granddaughter was spell bound, and with her eyes open wide, captivated, she hung on Grandfather's every word. "She found its frozen lifeless body lying on the cold ground one day. She gently scooped it up and cupped it gently in her hands and, with her warm breath, breathed the breath of life back into the fragile creature. After a time, the little bird came back to life and flew away, but it never ventured far. The little bird came to your grandma until the day it died at the threshold of the door."

"But she could bring it back to life again, right, Grandpa?"

"Well, sometimes we get second chances, but not always, and besides, your grandma wasn't there that time, unfortunately," he quietly reflected. "It was an extraordinary thing to watch, and I will remember it always."

"I wish I could have been there to see it, Grandpa," she lamented.

"I wish you could have been there too, little one."

The granddaughter realized, "She never told me."

"Doesn't like to brag about it, she's humble, so I tell her stories. Your grandma just does what she does."

The granddaughter begged, "Tell me more stories," and added, "See, Grandpa, she is magic."

"Yes, little one, I think she just may be magic." And he went on, "Did you know that she would always hang locks of her silky blond hair about the yard so the birds could build nests with it so she could be close to them and they could be close to her."

Granddaughter compared, "You have a lock of my hair, Grandpa. Remember I gave it to you?"

"Yes, I remember. So I could be close to you when you are far away."

"Maybe you could give it to the birds for their nests?"

"Yes, we could do that, but I was thinking of giving them some of mine too."

Granddaughter just looked at his bald head, giggled, and suggested, "We better use mine and Grandma's."

"Good idea." They laughed, and Grandpa went on about Grandma. "One time your grandma stopped me from saving a little yellow finch who had fallen into the fountain. It was struggling to climb out, but the sides were too steep."

"But why, Grandpa, did it drown?"

"Your grandma told her cat named Pickles to go and save the little bird."

"But, Grandpa, the cat would kill it. Cats eat birds," she protested.

"Grandma held me back and told me just to watch and not to interfere. I protested. She reaffirmed, 'Trust me.' The cat went over to the fountain and gingerly picked up the tiny bird in its mouth, placed it between its paws, and gently licked its feathers. After a time the cat stood up and backed away, and the little bird spread its wings and flapped, and it raised into the air, hesitating before the cat as if to thank her. And your grandfather knew that God himself had his hand on your grandma. I considered myself blessed to have witnessed such a remarkable thing."

And granddaughter just sat there and marveled for a moment, and then she jumped down off the swing and ran away, calling out as she left, "Bye, Grandpa."

"Don't you want to hear more stories?"

"No, it's okay, maybe later."

"Where are you going in such a hurry, little one?"

"To find Grandma."

"Why?"

"She might need my help in the garden and talk to the animals."

Grandfather just smiled and knew that she didn't want to miss one more magical moment with her grandma.

There was no inconsistency in doling out her love to the subjects who lived within the realm of her influence, nor was there incongruity in her respect for nature and her desire for balance in her garden kingdom, for she was wise and just.

He recalled the lesson of the butterfly who was hopelessly caught in the spider's web, wildly struggling to break free. "Aren't you going to save the butterfly?" he challenged.

"No, I can't, the spider must feed," she answered honestly. With concern, interest, and sobriety, they watched.

He reminded her, "But you saved the little finch that was drowning in the fountain."

"Honey," she said fondly, "this web belongs to the spider. I think of the fountain as my web, and it was my choice to save the finch. It was caught in my web."

"But the cat," I interrupted.

She smiled, "Yes the cat . . . you see, the cat knows well the order of things. Besides, it was my wish that the cat save the finch. I don't eat finches."

"I'm sure the cat does," I pointed out.

"Not that day," she affirmed.

"Lucky for the finch," he added. And he came to see things beyond that of the casual observer, as she generously shared the unseen secrets of her garden and revealed the true nature of things, for it was the language of nature in which she was most fluent.

Over time she developed an extraordinary lifelong bond with a family of blue jays and a special connection with one jay in particular. It was an event that would ultimately change everything. It all began when she saved a plump little fledgling who had fallen out of its nest one spring long ago. She was somehow able to discern the cries of the distressed parents who had flown down from their perch on the old weathered cedar fence in order to get her attention. At first the little bird was afraid, but with a little encouragement from his parents, she was finally able to coax the frightened little fledgling from behind the arborvitae hedge where it had fallen. "Don't worry, I'll take care of him for you," she assured the family, and she went on to nurse it back to health. After fixing a wing the little bird had broken from the fall and caring for the bird for a few days, she gently placed him back into the nest, instructing the parents, who were there to greet them, "Okay, here he is, all better now. I named him Blue, like the sky. Is that a good name?" The two parents just chirped and cocked their heads to the side and looked closely at her. "It's okay, you can go to him now." And the pair joined the fledgling, and they preened him while he happily chirped, telling them all about his ordeal.

Now as everyone knows, putting baby birds back into a nest after they have been touched by human hands is a risky business, and the chance of rejection is significant. The man was understandably concerned and challenged his wife, "Are you sure the birds will take the little one back?" But his wife affirmed that everything would be all right because she had talked to the parents of the bird and they understood everything. Still skeptical, the man held out, "Sounds like a fanciful children's story to me, where everything turns up roses and rainbows and happy endings."

"I'm sorry you are so cynical, dear. Miracles and good things can happen, and dreams can come true, only first you have to have faith and believe that they can happen."

There was no rejection that day; he witnessed what could only be described as yet another remarkable interaction between her and her beloved birds. Later on that day, as they sat in the garden, the pair of jays flew down and lightly sat in her lap and thanked her for what she had done; she softly spoke to them and stroked the top of their heads, and after moment's time, they flew off to take care of their young charge. Thereafter the jays would always bring her gifts, odd and sundry shiny things that they had found in their travels, and she would hang them on the willow tree every Christmas in honor of them.

And that certain jay she named Blue returned every season for some years after and became yet another permanent resident of the garden. And as was his nature, the man questioned, "And how do you know it's the same jay?"

She just looked at him and smiled and said, "Do you see that tiny locket around its neck?"

"Yes . . . I see it now."

"I placed it around his neck the day I put him back into the nest. He's had it on ever since that time."

"Really, I . . . never noticed."

"You don't notice a lot of things, Dad, and you miss so much. You need to be more observant."

The man's shoulders dropped a little, and he sank back into his wicker chair and sat in submissive silence, for she was absolutely right.

On one particular day, with their hands in the ground, garden-ing, she asked him, "Honey?"

"Yes, dear," he obliged.

She presented, "When I am not able to walk or get around anymore, will you promise to bring me out to my garden so I can enjoy my birds?"

"What brought that up?" he questioned.

"Oh, I was just thinking about the future, and we're getting older and it's harder to get around." He avoided answering her question and fell silent. She turned to face him and confirmed, "Honey, did you hear what I said?"

"Yes, I heard you," he admitted.

She was silent for a moment and then spoke again, "You know I love you so much, right?" He wondered what she was leading up to, and again he remained quiet. "There is one more thing, Dad. I've been thinking about it a lot, and it's really important to me . . ." she paused, and after a moment continued, "when I die, plant me here in the garden and let my body feed the flowers."

The man rose up and rested on his haunches and rejected, "What? No!"

She pursued her point, "I mean it, plant me here. Promise me, it's important."

He countered, "So now you can tell the future on top of everything else. And what makes you think or gives you the right to die before me? I'm sure you will live long beyond me. It's a fact that women live longer than men anyway."

"Maybe," she thought out loud as she stared at the soil in which here hands were deeply planted. She looked back at him with conviction. "It's my choice, you know." The man knew she was serious about it, and since she was his one weakness, he could never deny her anything she asked. He promised her that day to lay her to rest in her beloved garden. She followed with, "I love you, and I trust you. We have been together since the beginning of time. You are my poet, the love of my life. Now, I want to hear you say it. Promise me now, right here, right now." She grasped his arm with one hand and pointed to the ground in front of them with the other and directed, "Here, next to my beloved Daisymae." As she traced the name of her favorite dog etched deeply into the weathered stone, she gently related, "Daddy, did you know that *dog* is *God* spelled backwards?"

And he promised her, "You know I could never deny you anything. You know I love you more than my life, and you know that you're taking advantage of me right now. Yes, I promise."

She smiled, kissed him gently, and returned, "Thank you."

And the old man agonized over the somber conversation they had in the garden that day. Had she foretold the future? Could she really know the end from the beginning? And they settled into the river of time, got old, and never noticed, and there came a time late in life when his love fell out of the nest and broke her wing and she herself needed saving. She had a devastating stroke, which considerably altered her appearance. As a result, her face had fallen, and her features had become grotesque. She was not easily understood, as talking was laborious for her, and her words were mistaken for incoherent babble by others. And she forgot simple things, asking him the same question over and over again, and he would answer, not begrudgingly but for sympathy, for it was in concert with his own decline. He prayed for healing, which never came. He languished at the thought of not being able to bring the stone angels alive or build a path in their garden that that would lead them to the fountain of youth and of health. But alas, that was the nature of things, and they had no choice but to accept it; yet he would continue to deny and curse the cruel hand of nature. At long last they found themselves in the spider's web with no way out. There was no miracle in wait for her, no guardian of the wood, no angel in the garden to save her.

When she could no longer walk and was confined to a wheelchair, her beloved husband became her legs. In an attempt to give her some semblance of normalcy, he took her out of the house every week for years, to her favorite local café, where they had their meal and sat at the same out-of-the-way table that the restaurant owner had reserved specifically for them. And he would cut her meat for her and feed her and wipe her chin. He would take her hands in his and talk to her pleasantly, and she would listen intently, for she had further lost her ability to speak, so she spoke with her eyes, looking back at him longingly. And all that were in the restaurant would cast long, sorrowful looks their way. And the air was heavy with sadness and pity for her. And he would not cry; others would cry for him, for he saved his tears for her and shed them in private. What a good and decent man, what a prince of a man. And he recalled, while looking for purpose in his life, he was reminded by those close to him that, in time, he would come to know what it was and fulfil it, and it came down to this. One day the couple would not come to be there, and the other patrons noticed the table remained set, the Reserved sign still in place, the chairs in which they had sat remained empty and were carefully pulled up against the table, all for the couple who would never come again. They would be missed.

When Jane could no longer venture out beyond the house, she found what respite, joy, and peace she could in her garden. And as he had promised, every morning he would walk her outside into the garden, and her friends would come to greet her. And she would sit and visit there until she fell asleep. And again in the late afternoon, when the shadows grew long on the landscape, they would go out into her lovely garden and come to rest at her favorite spot in the courtyard, where a stone angel stood solemnly and waited for the passerby to join her in quiet reflection. And as he had done for so many times before, he placed her next to him, overlooking the bed of her favorite flowers, and sat down on the granite bench next to her. He swept her long platinum hair tossed by the breeze, back away from her face, and took her hand in his. He looked at her lovingly and remembered when they were young. And her dear jay, as he had every day for years, joined them there in that quiet place, and from his perch atop of the head of the angel, he watched her intently.

Now on that particular day, there was a certain chill in the air, and he carefully adjusted the shawl he had placed around her shoulders and smoothed out the blanket upon her lap. The old man trembled at the thought of what he found himself just now putting into words. Knowing she could not answer him, he conversed with himself and spoke while looking curiously at the jay, "Honey, how long do jays live anyway?" He knew it was impossible for jays to live so long, and it had already been some years. "Honey?" he repeated, and he gently squeezed her hand, which was cold to the touch. He denied, "It's okay, my love. You're tired, sleep now." And he was startled as the jay cried out with a squawk and flapped his wings and ascended into the sky above. And he followed him with his eyes and with his hand reached out to it as if to grasp it and bring it back. And he pleaded, "No, my friend, please stay. Please don't fly away . . . please." And he realized at that moment the love of his life was no more. The man was humbled, and he found his knees and laid his head in her lap and openly wept. He instinctively knew that her beloved Blue carried on his wings the very spirit of his love. And his heart was broken at that moment, and the stone angel watched and lamented.

He sat in silence, emotionless, numb. The funeral director placed a glass of water on the desk in front of the grieving old man. "How can I help you, sir?" the director kindly asked. The old man removed his cap and laid it in his lap. "It's my wife . . ."

"I'm sorry for your loss. What is her name?" the director replied.

"Jane," the man said flatly. "Her name is Jane," he repeated.

"Where is she?" the director wondered.

"Here, with me."

The director comforted the man and said, "We carry our loved ones in our hearts wherever we go."

"No," he protested, "she is here."

The director was confused and added, "Where?"

The man stood up and motioned for the director to follow him. The director pointed outside, and the man affirmed with a nod. The director followed the man outside to his car. After a moment's hesitation, the man opened the rear door of the car. He reached in and drew back the old patchwork quilt, which the family had warmed themselves with each and every Christmas, revealing the still form of his wife, lying in the back seat of his car as if asleep. The director looked at her and then at the man with sadness and placed his finger on her cold, lifeless neck for even a phantom pulse; he stepped back from the man. The director asked, "When did she die?"

"Yesterday . . . I think it was . . . yesterday."

He placed a hand on the man's shoulder and consoled, "I'm so very sorry." The director related, "It's okay, I will help you." Sensing the man had been through quite enough already, the director gently asked, "Have you called anyone?"

"Called . . . anyone," the man repeated blankly. The man stood and stared at the director, as if lost.

The director offered, "Perhaps her doctor. How about her family? Would you like me to call someone for you?"

"No, I am her family," the man said simply.

The director continued, "Did she have any last wishes?"

Without taking his eyes off his wife, the man addressed his wife softly, "Yes, Jane . . . there was something, wasn't there?" He remembered the promise he made to her.

The director interceded, "We need to put her where she belongs."

"I know," the man resigned gravely.

"Will you let me help you?"

The man just nodded.

The director prompted, "Why don't you come inside with me?"

The man just looked sorrowfully at his dead wife.

The director decided, "It's okay. You just stay right here. I'll be right back." The director placed a hand on the man's shoulder. "Are you sure you'll be okay?" The man nodded, and the director continued, "Yes, well, don't you worry. I'll take care of everything." When the director returned, the man was no longer there. He had left as mysteriously as he had come, and the mystery left with him. And the man returned home and fulfilled the promise he had made to his dear Jane.

After that, accompanied by sorrow and pain, his two remaining companions, the old man retired to the interior of the house, which held so many memories, and he closed the draperies and shut out the light, and it became the tomb in which he lost himself, and he lamented and he could not be comforted. For a long while no one came or went from the house. He became that very creature he loathed, bitter and angry, unfeeling and uncaring. He allowed the beautiful gardens the couple had spent a lifetime creating together fall into ruin; it became the outward manifestation of the decay that had crept into his soul.

He also closed out Christmas, and the stately willow tree, normally adorned with twinkling lights and bows and bells and garland

and ribbons and shiny ornaments, was dark. And that Christmas after his love had died, when the townspeople came to see and celebrate the tree, as they had done for many years, the light it had given to everyone was no more, and there was a profound sadness in the town.

And it was early the following Christmas morning when there came an unexpected tapping at the window, and it startled the man, who was quietly sitting in the darkness. The man tried to ignore the annoying tapping, but the caller was insistent. The man rose up out of his chair and went to the window. He threw back the draperies to reveal a familiar jay. And the man mocked, "Oh, it's you." He opened the door, leaned out, and announced, "You left us, remember? That day in the garden? And now you return to torment me. Go away and leave me be. There's nothing for you here." As he closed the door on the jay, he charged, "Torment me no longer, bird." And the man returned to his chair; but before he could sit down, the tapping began again at the window. The determined jay remained, demanding an audience with the man. Again the man got up and went to the door and coarsely directed, "What do you want from me? You're too late, she's dead, she's gone. Don't you know?" He stepped out onto the porch and pressed, "Now shoo, go on now and leave me. Pesky bird anyway." The jay turned and flew off in the direction of the willow tree, and the man watched and called after the bird, "Good riddance."

Just then, a curious, wonderful thing happened; as the jay landed on a branch of the tree, the entire tree seemed to come alive with the squawks and flapping wings of hundreds of jays, as they burst into the air all at once, flying off in all directions. The old man was surprised and wiped his eyes in disbelief. And the tree exploded, in a puff of feathers, fluff, and fluttering foul. And as the last of the floating feathers fell and settled on the ground, the old man finally saw the willow tree, decorated with bright ribbons and strings and shiny things, and the breeze moved the branches and it sparkled in the morning light, and it was beautiful. The jay rejoined the man on the porch. The man was stunned, and he turned to the jay and asked, "You . . . did this for her, for us?" The jay cocked its head to the side, eyeing him closely. With the palm of his hand up, the man reached out to the jay and the jay leapt onto his arm and placed in his open hand the very locket that his dear wife had placed around the neck of the young jay she had saved so many years ago. "Thank you, little jay." And the jay chirped, and the man repeated, "No . . . thank you, from the bottom of my heart." And the man opened his heart to the bird and for the first time called him Blue, the name given him by his guardian. "I was a fool, with no eyes to see with . . . can you . . ." and the jay flew up and away, squawking as it flew. The man thought, "Was it all just a dream?" and then he looked down at the locket, for it was real. And he stumbled on the step and slid down the pole he was hanging on to, and he sat down on the step of the porch, and with his arms wrapped around the post, he gazed in amazement at the weeping willow tree. The tree, which nature had so generously decorated, had once again taken on the mantle of Christmas. And an overwhelming peace poured into the man and changed him that day, and he saw things more clearly now, for his tears washed the lenses of his eyes.

And the man came back from that time long ago to the present, there at the Laundromat. As he rose up out of his chair and take his leave, the man next to him held his arm and asked, "Aren't you going to stay to see what happens?"

"I already know, my friend, and so do you," and he left. The man didn't have to look back to see what was about to happen. He all along knew, for the birds who were called by this old woman would descend out of the sky at precisely the time they were supposed to. He also knew that birds are free spirits, and they don't just happen by, for as is the case with angels, they are called, and sometimes they interfere in human affairs for good. The angel that came to minister to the man that Christmas morning came simply in the form of a little bird named Blue. And as his love reminded, "the good done to them always comes back to you."

And the event changed the man, and he once again started to live and believe in the future. He returned the garden to its former glory and became the guardian of it. As he sat by himself in the garden, he was not alone. The unmistakable presence and spirit of his beloved Jane moved in and about the garden. And the man was never without the company of the faithful, loyal blue jay, who continued to visit him there, perched on the head of the stone angel. And the jay raised generations in that garden.

And he sat back in his wicker chair in the garden, closed his eyes, and went back to where it all began, back to that small town, in an unremarkable house, at the end of the lane, where he and his dear Jane loved and lived a lifetime and raised their family, which extended beyond them for generations, and she grew her garden and gave sanctuary to the many creatures that lived there. It was their home, it was their heaven—it was their creation.

(by Darrell W. McNabb, 2017)

The Tale of the Wayward Travelers

> *I was hungry and you gave me food, I was thirsty and you gave me a drink, I was a stranger and you took me in.*
>
> —Matthew 25:35

It was Christmas again, and as was our tradition, our family would gather together on Christmas Day, where we would bathe in the warmth of each other's company and celebrate the spirit of this blessed season. After the exchanging of gifts, partaking in a bountiful meal and assorted spirits, now filled with the festivities of the day, we all retired to the comfort of the living room. My son and I settled down into two easy chairs before the fire. After a time, Bill leaned forward and opened a conversation with, "Dad, there is one last gift under our tree that I'm hoping you can help me unwrap." This was curious, must be something special.

"Indeed a surprise," I followed.

Bill responded, "More like a mystery." He presented an opened envelope with a card protruding from it and handed it over and directed me to read it.

"Looks like you don't need any help opening it," I offered. I paused and studied the envelope. "An envelope with no return address on it, curious."

"That's right, Dad, no return address."

"What is it anyway, a Christmas card or something?"

"Or something," Bill added. "I was hoping you could tell me."

"Grandma, fetch my glasses please," I directed.

She looked over and said, "Check your collar."

"Oh, there they are," I claimed.

"Where they always are, dear," Grandma reminded and remarked, "Your dad needs glasses to find his glasses."

I placed my glasses on my face, carefully removed the card from the envelope, and read aloud, "To our angels—the McNabbs." I stopped and laid the card in my lap and quietly repeated, "To our angels—the McNabbs." I removed my glasses and wiped my eyes, which were wet with tears.

"Dad, what's wrong?" Bill queried.

"Where did you get this?" I questioned.

"In the mail. I thought that maybe you had sent it."

I sat back and reflected, "They had found us, and after all this time."

Bill asked, "What do you mean, they found us?"

"I have a story to tell you, son."

"And I am listening," he implored.

"I recall it's been, what, over fifty years ago now. It's about your grandfather. Of course you're familiar with the expression 'What comes around, goes around' and the 'pay it forward' concept."

"Of course, Dad, but what's that got to do with it?"

"It has everything to do with it."

Bill sat up well forward on his chair and anxiously awaited the telling of this tale, and I began.

*   *   *

In a seemingly unending procession of predictable days, this day in late November began like so many others for this man and his family. I recall my father, your grandfather, waking in the early dawn, greeted only by winter's chill, as he headed out into the thick fog to meet that well-worn road that led him away to work. It was a tiresome, tedious journey that he made day after day for many years. The road he traveled was a rough broad band of asphalt, resembling a great black river, and like an arrow, it cut straight through the center of the fertile San Joaquin Valley, stretching the entire length of the great valley from the windswept summit of the grapevine in the south to the gates of the mountains far to the north. The inland highway was the main thoroughfare along the West Coast, connecting all the small townships that lined its banks, continuously moving commerce and sweeping the thousands of weary travelers along its length.

With Dad launched and on his way, Mom was not far behind him. She raised us from our long winter's nap and pressed us to get moving, as we all had pressing appointments with life, places to go and things to do. In a flurry of activity, the three children, ranging in age from seven to ten, hurried along by our mother, frantically readied themselves for school. When the dust settled, then bundled and bridled, with a lunch pail in hand, a kiss from Mom and an open door, one after the other we filed out of the house and scurried out into the world and off to school.

Those were the days of stay-at-home moms—moms whom we associate with love, comfort, safety, warmth, stability, and peace. While everything in our world seemed to move and change from moment to moment, only Mom remained constant, fixed in our universe, and our lives revolved around her. It was nice to know that Mom was always there, keeping the home fires burning, holding everything together. She poured herself into the family—it was her focus, her passion in life, her career, and not a day goes by that I am not thankful for her strength and her perseverance.

As the day wound down and each of us accomplished our missions out in the world, we again returned home from school to a warm greeting from Mom to finish the day where it began. With great haste we dispatched our chores, wrapped up our homework, and reconvened in the kitchen, where Mom was busy preparing supper. Met with hunger and attracted by the overwhelming aroma of freshly baked bread and a roast beast cooking in the oven, armed with forks and spoons, we began going from pot to pan, sampling, Mom all the while swatting us away as if we were pesky flies. We were not so easily dissuaded, and Mom sternly warned, "I don't care if you're hungry. You'll just have to wait till your father gets home."

With few exceptions, the family of the fifties always sat down at the table and ate supper together. It was the one time of the day when everyone could meet together as a family, share the events of the day, and dwell on other more important matters. We looked forward to the bonding time and that sense of unity and belonging that our time together fostered.

Dad, who had left very early that morning, had not yet returned home. It was highly irregular for our father to come home so late, and while Mom was becoming anxious, we were becoming impatient. We sat around the kitchen table and stared at the plastic rooster clock that hung on the wall, fixated on it, as though we could move it forward with our minds. Mom displayed some growing concern as she thought to herself aloud, "Now I wonder where your father could be." He normally arrived home from work by 5:30 p.m., and we would all be seated at the table eating by 6:00. It was now pushing seven o'clock and still no word from Dad; Mom's concern turned to worry.

As Mom paced around the kitchen, fussing over the cookery, we took up our vigilant watch at the wide front-room window where we all perched in line upon the broad sill like three oversize knickknacks, and there we waited for the arrival of that moss green '54 Plymouth sedan, which would deliver my dad and signal the time to eat.

It wasn't long before our vigilance was rewarded as the lights of his car flashed in the glass of the window, and we would run to the door in anticipation. Now anticipating Dad's arrival wasn't always met with enthusiasm—for instance, if I had got into trouble that day, and Mom had delivered something on the order of, "You just wait until your father gets home," I would have been scarce indeed.

Immediately upon Dad's arrival, we all raced from the window to the front door, pushing and shoving, falling over each other to be the first to greet Father. We swung the door open wide and held it fast in preparation for his entrance. We were totally surprised as Dad was not alone; he had an entourage of no less than five other figures traipsing behind him. "Hi, kids," Dad said as he entered, and we mauled him, that is, until he'd had enough. He pushed the rest of the way through the opening, and little by little we shuffled backward to make room for the group.

As they all stepped inside, out of the damp cold and came into the light, I counted three children, a man, and a woman. I closed the door behind them and quickly joined my brother and sister, who were standing there, eyeing the strangers, sizing them up as it were. They reminded me of a small flock of timid sheep, as they stood huddled together just inside the door behind Dad.

Mom called from the kitchen, "Bill, is that you?"

"Mom, Dad's home!" we followed in unison. As Mom entered the front room from the kitchen, wiping her hands on her apron, she charged, "You're home late tonight. What happened to you anyway? Dinner's been ready for more than an hour it's probably cold now, and—" she abruptly stopped in midsentence. Turning an inquisitive smile, Mom tritely spoke, "And, who's this?" She joined us in the awkward moment, and together we stood and anxiously awaited an explanation about the group of strangers he was standing in front of.

Making no apologies about being late, Dad jumped in, "Lois, kids, these are some friends I found out on the highway on my way home tonight."

I thought to myself, It's not like a stray dog or something, Dad, you just pick up and bring home. They meekly and jointly offered, "Hello." Now Dad's use of the word *friends* puzzled me. I knew most of his friends and maintained that these people were strangers. Dad went on, "They are on a trip out here from back east and were just passing through, when their car broke down. I stopped to help and well . . . here we are."

"And here you are," Mom echoed.

Dad added, looking for concurrence from Mom, "I figured they could come to our house and at least have dinner, and maybe stay till they can get back on the road. I said you would be fine with it, Lois."

Following Dad's lead, Mom cordially offered, "Of course they can stay. You're welcome to stay with us. Please, come in."

Later, I would overhear Mom privately challenge Dad's resolve on the matter, referring to him as a Good Samaritan and reminding him, while that is all well and good, to remember that charity begins at home. She suggested that he could have just as easily taken the family to a motel or a garage to get their car fixed, and expressed concern over not having prepared enough food and where they all would sleep in our small house. Dad claimed we'll share; we'll make do with what we have, like we always have in the past. Dad protested that the repair might take some time and that they didn't know anybody and had kids with them, to which Mom volleyed, "You also have a family at home, who was worried sick about you."

"I know, I know," he resigned.

Mom knew that Dad couldn't just leave the family stranded there on the side of the road cold and hungry, also realizing that we could have been those people. Of course Dad's arguments were right and just, and Mom saw the truth in it.

Now many would not have done what my dad did, I suspect out of inconvenience or most likely fear. My sense is that my dad's upbringing in those lean years he spent in Oklahoma back in the thirties, during and following the dust bowl, while it decimated his family financially, it strengthened his desire to reach out to the less fortunate, give them a hand, and help them get them back onto their feet. It was this character from which the man could not be separated, this man with whom my mother fell in love so long ago.

And so Dad made the introductions, and for the short time they were with us, we weaved their family into the fabric of ours.

Now Mom was quite the expert at stretching both food and accommodations, as over the years, visitors and relations from near and far would drop by our house unexpectedly; it seemed to me that our house became a mecca for wayward travelers. Mom always welcomed any and all at her table, and she turned no one away. Once again, she applied her magic, and we all sat down together for supper and ate and drank our fill and were satisfied. The kids played silly games and engaged in other nonsense until they eventually succumbed to slumber and were tucked away for the night. The adults engaged in conversation far into the night until their words waned, and finally, with a yawn and a good night, they wandered off into the room Mom had earlier prepared for them. The woman paused, turned to my mom, and profusely apologized for the intrusion, no doubt understanding the position her family had put them in. My mother was graceful and assured the woman that they were neither an inconvenience, nor were they an imposition, and she added that the entrance to her home like her heart was, and had always been, a revolving door. Wiping a tear from her cheek, the woman reached out, warmly embraced my mom, thanked her, and retired for the night. Over the years many, by chance or by choice, ended up in the lap of Mom's hospitality and have been richly blessed by it.

We all shared what we had with the family; they stayed the night with us and became those friends we hadn't met, that long-lost family we only rediscovered. In a short time we forgot they were strangers that had invaded our house but a few hours before.

Early the following day, while it was still dark and while everyone slept, Dad silently left on a mission. On this day he departed from his normal routine; he took time off from work, contacted the owner of a local garage, and had the man's car towed and repaired. It's important to note here that my dad never took a day off from work in his life, and as far as the repair on the family's car, Dad took on the expense of the repair himself without a second thought about it.

To everyone's surprise, Dad returned later that morning with the family's car repaired and ready to carry them on the rest of their journey. The people offered my parents money for their trouble, which they predictably refused. The people asked my folks how they could ever repay them for their kindness, insisting, "Are you sure there isn't something, anything that we can do for guys?" Dad assured the couple, knowing they were okay and safely on their way was payment enough. I see it as sort of an investment Dad made on his own future welfare that day as he paid forward. After thinking about it, Mom added, "There is one thing you could do."

"Just name it," they excitedly followed.

Mom finished, "Remember us, and drop us a line just to let us know you got home okay." They promised they would write, and Dad and Mom said that they would look forward to hearing from them, although I suspect that it wasn't an expectation and wouldn't hold them to it. As we said goodbye to the family that day, we all embraced no longer as strangers but as friends.

As the family drove away, I reflected how close people can become in the space of a fortnight; and I am reminded that it is those lasting bonds of friendship, which remain rooted in humble beginnings, the result of some chance encounter along life's path.

Dad and Mom knew their acts of kindness and caring also held a deeper intrinsic value—they knew that the good deed they performed would most certainly be proliferated and that their children would always carry with them the lessons of this day.

A few months had passed since our guests had left our company, and Christmas was once again upon us. And in addition to the other presents placed under our tree that year, there was one other gift, just one other. The travelers were as good as their word, for that Christmas, a card and a letter with a heartfelt message arrived from them, thanking my folks for their kindness. The letter began, "To our angels, the McNabb family." It made me proud to be thought of in this way. After reading it aloud to the family, Mom turned the envelope over, noticing, "Bill, there's no return address on the card." I recall they just looked at each other and understood that the gift they had given so openly had been returned to them, to us; and it was a way to let us know that they were out there somewhere safe and that they would never forget what my parents did for them that one cold winter's night.

And the next Christmas, and every Christmas after, there came a simple card addressed simply "to Our Angels—the McNabbs."

I recall the cards came for some years after, and then sadly, one day they stopped coming, and we feared that something had happened to our friends, yet we hoped and trusted they were okay. We have long since moved away from the little town; however, that precious memory moved with us. Even years later, it was never very far from our minds, and with fondness, we thought about them. And I often thought about the time we moved over and made room in our home and in our hearts for others, and the many blessings we have received because of the unselfish, caring actions of my mother and father so long ago.

*   *   *

Upon finishing the tale at our place by the fire, I turned to Bill and closed, "You know, Bill, I held on to this memory for many years, until the memory no longer visited me, and then one day I had forgotten about it altogether."

"Until now," Bill clarified.

"Until now," I concurred.

Having taken the tale to that quiet, reflecting place deep within himself, where fond memories reside, Bill reflected in silence for some moments, and when words returned to him, he said, "I, don't know what to say. It's a beautiful, extraordinary story."

"It's a Christmas story, it's our story," I added. And as we continued to stare into the fading fire light, which flamed and flickered and danced upon the walls and animated our faces, our conversation waned and we sat in silent thought. Finally, late was the hour when shadows fell in the room and dreams would call on us to join them; Bill slowly rose out of his deep chair, gently placed a hand on my shoulder, and softly spoke, "Thank you, Dad, for everything . . . I love you. Merry Christmas."

I placed my hand on his and answered, "Merry Christmas to you, son."

He wandered off to bed, and I lingered in front of the dying fire and eventually drifted off to sleep and dreamed about former days and Christmases long past.

It is clear to me that where one's circumstances and means preclude their ability to give material things, there are no limits on gifts from the heart, which venture far above and beyond all of one's other resources. The great and grand generosity of God is Christmas, the gift of a child delivered to us one silent night in humble estate, an act of love and caring, which reverberates through generations and echoes in eternity and which is embedded in the spirit of every soul.

Know that the deeds of our fathers and the blessings that follow will be remembered and realized by some future generation, in some future time.

(by Darrell W. McNabb, 2013)

The Man Who Came to Dinner

Be careful what you wish for, for you may get it.
—A version of the saying from a Spanish
proverb, attributed to St. Teresa of Avila
(1895) and the writings of Aesop (550 BC)

On a rocky outcropping on the edge of the great Pacific Ocean, they stood together arm in arm, two old souls watching the advancing tide roll in, once again reclaiming the shoreline. They breathed in the cold, salty air, and Lucy's silvery blond hair, touched by time, whipped about in the wind. In a series of waves, one after the other the expanse of cold water relentlessly moved farther and farther inward toward them, eventually swallowing the exposed beach.

"Life is like that, isn't it, dear?" Carl reflected aloud as he looked on at the advancing tide. He turned to Lucy and sought confirmation. "Know what I mean?"

Breaking away from her fixation on the ocean that lay before them, Lucy numbly responded, "I'm sorry, what did you say, Daddy?"

Carl redirected, "Life is like a tide that comes in waves until it covers everything." Carl looked back out at the sea and went on, "Remember I almost drowned once, in the rising tide."

"And the strong current," Lucy added and went on, "Remember—how could I forget? I almost lost you that day. You were out there alone, and I couldn't do anything to help you. You know, Daddy, I told you not to stay out there so long by yourself. I don't care how good of a swimmer you are, or were, you could still get into trouble."

"I know. I struggled to get back to the beach," Carl confirmed, and reflected, "I couldn't gain my footing or catch my breath. The ocean can be so unforgiving, but then that's just the nature of things. But I still somehow found a way back to shore."

"To me," Lucy celebrated, as she tightened her grip on Carl.

"To you," Carl agreed as he looked deeply, lovingly into her eyes.

Lucy added, "Carl, you know that together we can endure anything." Lucy knew that Carl was an excellent swimmer and that it was a very dangerous situation, even for him. It was an all too familiar scenario that had claimed the lives of other very strong swimmers in the past, as sometimes there was no escape. Believing that Carl's surviving the experience was more than luck or clear thinking, Lucy pressed, "How did you make it, Daddy, when others didn't?"

Carl explained simply, "I stopped trying to fight it, swam back out to sea, and came back in somewhere else on the beach."

Lucy reminded, "You told me that you panicked and asked God for help."

Leaving God out of the equation, fishing for just the right way to say it, Carl acknowledged, "Well, I started to panic, but then I found my wits and became calm. I thought I was going to drown that day."

Lucy consoled, "Why don't you ever admit you need help? There's nothing wrong with that, you know. It doesn't make you less of a man. You're only human." Lucy continued, "You think you can fix everything. You just can't . . . you're not God, and whether you believe it or not, I believe God was there that day, for you, for us. Sometimes you just need his help."

Carl resigned, "I know, but I put myself in that predicament, not God."

Lucy paused and assured, "You know that I love you. I have always loved you, and I always will."

Carl followed, "No matter what?"

"No matter what," Lucy concluded.

Referring to their own experiences in life, Carl recalled, "We spent our time in life's ocean together, didn't we, dear?"

"Yes, we did," Lucy reassured.

"And here we are still—we survived together," Carl claimed. "We were meant to survive, Lucy." They were old now and considered themselves blessed to be able to look back on their close calls, remembering their time of rising tides.

Over the course of our lives, all of us will go through a time of rising tides, to some degree or another—a difficult, challenging time, when there aren't enough resources, not enough food, friends, or money; a rough patch of life marked by illness, injury, or even death; a family crisis or some other unseen hardship. These times may arrive without warning and oftentimes visit the unsuspecting in a progression of overwhelming waves. As the old, timeless, and ever-relevant adage suggests, "when it rains, it pours." Unsure what to do, where to turn, having our best-laid plans scattered, we may actually reach that breaking point. Ultimately, the very foundation of our faith is tested, our character measured, and out of the ensuing desperation of the situation, we ultimately concede that nothing short of a prayer or a miracle would save us.

Yet we reason that surely calm must follow calamity, just as prosperity and peace must follow upheaval, and at the end of a path of certain disaster, the possibility of a favorable end may greet us still. And if we persevere and hope and pray, might some good prevail out of a bad beginning—that if the ways be departed from, and the course corrected, that the bonds of misfortune that bind us to this course be loosed, not always, or more particularly, not in the sense we think it should.

This is where the young family found themselves, chasing hope, which was fast setting on their horizon, not remembering how they got there or perceiving a way out. And so, like storm clouds, the waves of the ocean of life lined up, and one after the other, they proceeded to slam into the young family.

It was at that time not more than a month before Christmas that Lucy had lost her job of many years. It was a job that she had counted on. Lucy's income was essential for the struggling family, especially since her husband had fallen critically ill and had been unable to work for some time now. Past conveyance from the company to Lucy regarding her value, appreciation for her years of service and her loyalty was of little consolation now, as she sat silently in her car, on the edge of tears, staring at the layoff notice, which briefly stated, "Your services are no longer required." It was clear that the economic downturn sweeping the country had hit home in the most personal way.

As the reality of the situation set in, Lucy wondered what the family would do. Where would they go from here, and how would she tell her husband the news? She thought about Carl, Bill, and their youngest child, Mark. Lucy considered that she and her husband had always weathered the storm before and that there was nothing they couldn't endure or overcome together.

A short time after Carl completed Mortuary College the previous year, he contracted an active case of a drug-resistant strain of tuberculosis from a body he had embalmed. Although contracting this type of disease from a dead body was possible, it was, however, unusual; and for the better part of a year, as his family stood by ever vigilant, Carl struggled with an advanced case of the disease, which at one point nearly claimed his life. He spent eight months in quarantine, receiving multiple doses of experimental chemical therapy drugs, and after a long period of convalescence, Carl eventually recovered.

Because of the long-term illness, Carl was unable to work during that time. Coupled with the advent of Lucy losing her job, things were looking grim for the family financially, as they were now plagued with the lack of income. In addition to Carl's residual medical costs and student loans, which had piled up, the couple had also fallen two months behind on their rent payment, which they were struggling to keep up with. They found themselves well into December and were now at the mercy of their landlord; of course Lucy would do the only thing she could do at this point and pleaded with the landlord for leniency. Finally able to work, Carl had just started looking for a job, and with Christmas just twelve days before them, the timing could not have been worse. Things weren't looking good for the family, and as life happens, things got worse, as yet another unforeseen, unfortunate pitfall befell them—it was yet another log on the bonfire of the family's mounting affliction.

Their youngest son, Mark, had recently become critically ill as a cold slipped into bronchitis and further progressed into pneumonia. Lucy and Carl had initially taken him into emergency for treatment, where the resident doctor diagnosed Mark's condition as a bad cold and sent the couple away. Mark's condition quickly deteriorated, and they returned to the emergency room again the following day. At the insistence of Lucy and Carl, a more thorough examination revealed that he had pneumonia. Realizing Mark was considerably worse than previously thought, another doctor immediately referred them to the hospital admitting. Because the couple did not have insurance due to their unemployed status, the hospital refused to admit the sick boy; they were turned away from the hospital a second time and instructed to treat him at home. Deeply disappointed, the couple returned home with their critically ill son.

After discovering her personal doctor, whom she had normally taken her son to since his birth, had recently been disbarred, convicted of a medical malpractice, he had since closed the door on his practice, leaving no referral for his many ailing patients. Lucy contacted several pediatricians in the area, to no avail. Now desperate for help, Lucy turned to a longtime friend, Alice, to whom she confided everything. Alice referred Lucy to her pediatrician. At this point, Lucy was skeptical, having been turned away so often; she reminded Alice again of the couple's lack of insurance and questionable ability to pay for services, which seemed to be the undermining issue preventing them securing help. Alice assured Lucy, that the doctor would help them regardless, that he was a good, compassionate man, and that she could trust him and that he would understand their situation.

Hopeful, Lucy followed up with a call to Dr. Freeman for help, realizing all the while she would be asking for charity as she was unable to pay him at this point.

The voice on the other end of the phone stated briefly that "the doctor is not taking on new patients at this time." Lucy felt like she had been hit in the chest with a hammer. She pleaded with the voice on the other end of the phone, "But you don't understand, my son will die without treatment."

The receptionist on the phone suggested taking her son to the hospital for emergency care. With what little composure she had left, now frustrated and emotional, Lucy rapidly related her story. After a brief pause, the now all too familiar response came, "I'm sorry, I wish I could help you. However, I can give you a referral . . . please hold."

Lucy jumped in to the empty phone, "But I can't . . . I am running, out of time. Hello, hello!" Lucy's heart sank as she heard the dial tone as the phone disconnected. Desperate to help her son, she continued to hold the phone up close to her ear, and with tears in her eyes, she continued to plead with the silence. Without hanging up, Lucy set it down on the table next to her, where she sat forward and numbly waited, as if she expected some miracle to occur. She openly wept, and she prayed and pleaded, "God, please help me. Please, God, it's my son . . . my son . . . please." At that very moment, Lucy heard a man's voice coming from the phone. She looked down at the phone in disbelief, for the phone clearly did not ring and had been disconnected. Lucy quickly snatched it off the table and excitedly insisted, "Hello, hello," she repeated.

The voice came back, "Mrs. Williams, this is Dr. Freeman, how can I help you?"

"I'm Lucy, Lucy Rosenthal, and—"

"Excuse me just a moment," Dr. Freeman proposed, as he held the phone away and insisted, "Mary, I thought you had Mrs. Williams for me on line 2?"

"She was, but apparently she hung up," Mary answered.

Dr. Freeman ordered, "Please get her back on the phone. I need to talk to her." Dr. Freeman returned to the phone with Lucy, "I'm sorry, there must have been some sort of mistake here. I'll have Mary straighten this out."

Lucy clung to the voice and pleaded, "No, wait, please. It's no mistake, no mistake. Please help me, Doctor."

Sensing her desperation, Dr. Freeman spoke, assuring Lucy, "Lucy?"

"Yes, Doctor," Lucy followed. "Just give me one moment," and further emphasized, "Please, don't hang up." Lucy then heard the doctor firmly order, "Mary, please hold my other calls and transfer this one to my office."

As the doctor returned to Lucy, he opened, "Yes, Lucy, how can I help you?"

"Thank you, God!" Lucy exclaimed.

"Dr. Freeman will do," he clarified.

Lucy excitedly returned, "Yes . . . well . . . I meant that . . . you're a godsend, doctor. I know you're busy, and thank you, thank you so much for taking my call." And Lucy went on to tell the doctor everything, scarcely stopping to breathe. The doctor understood the deep level of frustration and the sense of urgency in her voice. Lucy pressed the phone to her ear, jumping right over what just happened and, in a trembling voice, quickly told him the whole story, to which he quietly and thoughtfully listened. At one point Lucy stopped in midsentence, afraid of losing the only caring voice in her universe, and asked the doctor, "Doctor? Are you still there?" To which he patiently answered, "Yes, I am still here with you. Please, go on." Lucy finally finished, "And that's it, Doctor. I don't know what to do. You are my last hope."

And the doctor, with whom Lucy and Carl later became inseparable friends until his death some years later, intervened and personally managed Mark's care. Because of their lack of insurance, inability to pay him, and the refusal of the hospital to hospitalize their son, the primary care of the boy had incidentally fallen into the laps of Lucy and Carl. They became full-time nurses at home under the direction of the doctor. Following a visit to the family's home, reaching into his own resources, the doctor had taken it upon himself to procure and personally pay for a large portion of the necessary medication. In an extremely uncommon act of generosity and kindness, Dr. Gerald Freeman further told Lucy that he would not charge them at the time and that he would work something out with the couple when they got on their feet financially. In the meantime, it was the doctor's express order to Lucy and Carl to concentrate on the health of their son. It was an extraordinary stroke of fortune for the struggling family, coming at the time they most needed it.

Despite the positive turn of events and the blessings bestowed on the family by the physician, the path to reclaim the health of their youngest son was not an easy one, as it was fraught with challenges. Unfortunately, Mark got worse before he got better, testing the couple's resolve at every turn. Lucy cried and prayed and remained ever vigilant as she tended the listless boy day and night. In his unwavering commitment to the child's health, the doctor and their friend stood with the family during their time of need, providing his unwavering support until Mark was fully recovered and again healthy. In hindsight, Lucy and Carl knew that it was indeed providential that they had not been working at the time their son was critically ill; they would not have been able to devote the time necessary to care for him.

The mood was particularly somber when Carl solemnly walked through the front door of their home that evening. The joy that the family had known had gone, and it was cold and quiet in the house. Carl walked down the hall and found his wife in Mark's room, which was dimly lit, standing at the foot of the crib of her precious infant son, where she had been keeping an ever-vigilant watch on the still form on the bed. Carl put his arm around her gently, and she melted into him. "How is he today?" he asked softly. Taking the tone of hopefulness, he continued, "Getting better I'm sure," he answered his question. "Have you eaten?" Carl asked Lucy.

She just looked up at him with glassy, sorrowful eyes, and she cried, "Your TB, losing my job, the house, and now this. Oh, Carl, what are we going to do? It seems like the world is fighting against us."

Carl gently pressed, "Come on, let's get something to eat. You'll feel better . . . please, for me. Where is Bill? It's so quiet."

"He's in his room, making decorations for our Christmas tree, which we don't have, and I have no idea what present we can get for him to put beneath it if we did. You know, Carl, he's been so good through all this." Now Lucy had been crying, betrayed by swollen, puffy eyes, and was spent from a day of seemingly useless energies.

Carl redirected Lucy with a nod in the direction of the kitchen. Lucy consented, and arm in arm they walked down the hallway and toward the kitchen. They made it to the living room, where they sat down together. They looked at each other and silently contemplated. In the face of plenty, it's easy to forget where you came from, but how could they forget.

Replying to Carl's earlier question, Lucy solemnly spoke, "He's not good, Carl. It was a bad day. He couldn't keep anything down. He vomited over and over again. Just when it seems like he's making some progress, he gets worse."

"Did you call the doctor?" Carl asked.

"I've been on the phone with him, most of the day. He said he is going the right direction and that he needs to get the fluid out of his lungs and he would check in with us tomorrow, and to call him right away if the vomiting continues. He said to allow the medicine to take effect. He will get better, but he would come to the house if need be. The doctor seems confident, must know something we don't. I'm scared that we'll lose our son." Looking for consolation, Lucy implored, "He'll get better, he'll be alright, won't he, Carl?"

Carl validated, "I mean, he's the doctor, right? He knows what he's doing. We have to have faith in him. Mark will be okay, you'll see. It's just going to take a while, like he said."

Lucy asked, "Any luck on finding a job?"

"I have a couple of prospects, just waiting for a call," Carl said, conflicted, not wanting to burden Lucy further, but he didn't want to hide the fact there was something else he had to tell her; he added, "Actually, I was lucky to make it home today."

"What do you mean?" Lucy queried.

"The car's acting up again. It died a couple of times on the way home. Don't know if it will start again tomorrow."

Lucy sat back deep into the couch, her morale now completely deflated. It wasn't hard to read Lucy's fading morale as Carl validated, "I know, Lucy, you don't have to tell me. I can see it by the look on your face."

Again Lucy pleaded, "What are we going to do, Carl? We can't seem to catch a break."

Carl wrapped her in his arms and assured, "We continue to persevere, that's what we do, soldier on, and pray if you need to, something will break. You'll see . . . always does, right?"

Lucy backed away from Carl and directed, "How do we do that, with what? Maybe . . . it's a punishment for something we've done or not done." Lucy reflected and went on, "Carl, why don't you pray with me right now."

"I can't," Carl answered tritely.

"You can't, or you won't," Lucy volleyed and continued, "You know, Carl. It's like you don't believe in God or something."

"I believe God helps those who help themselves," Carl entreated.

Lucy followed solemnly, "I don't know about this time, Daddy. It . . . it feels different somehow . . . darker, and there seems to be no way out. And besides, it's easy for you to say 'it will all work out and be okay,' when I'm the one who lives with it, day after day." Lucy went on to challenge Carl, "You don't cry or feel or seem to worry. You don't show any emotion at all. How can you be so calm when everything in our world seems to be falling apart around us?"

Carl defended, "I don't show it. You cry for me. I weep on the inside."

"That's just not fair," Lucy wept.

Carl comforted, "You're right, life isn't fair. Look, I just know that things will be okay. They will turn out the way they are supposed to. I'm here with you. We're in this together, no matter what."

"I don't know how you can be so confident," Lucy questioned.

Carl cradled Lucy's face in his hands and offered, "I know you need me here now, and you know that I need you. We need to be strong. I wish I could be here with you all the time. You know I'm trying to find a job. That is my job now, Lucy, to find a job as soon as I can . . . and I will, okay?"

Lucy nodded and resigned, "Okay."

Carl disconnected from Lucy, stood up, and walked into kitchen. "What's for dinner?"

"Soup," Lucy answered.

"Soup, uh . . . that's all we ever have any more—soup. I want something with substance. I'm sure we've got something else besides soup," Carl charged.

"Crackers and some cheese, I think. Look for yourself," Lucy followed as she joined Carl in the kitchen and illustrated to him, as she opened the empty refrigerator and one cupboard door after another, exposing bare shelves.

"We have to go shopping, Lucy," Carl announced.

"With what, Carl, our good looks? This is not helping, Carl."

"What's not helping?" Carl asked.

"Going on like this," Lucy added.

Carl found a small whole chicken in the freezer and pointed out, "What about this?"

"I was saving that for our Christmas dinner, which is just three days from now," Lucy punctuated.

"Well, don't know about the rest of you, but that's enough for me," Carl smiled.

Lucy sat silent, unmoved by Carl's attempt to lighten up the moment. He went on, "That's a joke, Lucy, just a joke."

"It's not funny, Carl," Lucy followed seriously.

"I know, Lucy. It isn't at all. Look, I know you're tired of living like this. I know I am," Carl finished. Lucy sat down at the kitchen table and with her silence agreed with him.

Carl joined his wife at the table. Lucy took Carl's hands in hers and suggested, "Why don't we ask the church or the Salvation Army for some help? What about friends, your family. How about your parents?"

"I can't . . . you know I won't," Carl snapped back.

"Damn your pride, Daddy, it won't feed us," Lucy fired back. She continued, "It's like a self-imposed poverty, Carl. What are you trying to prove anyway? Why don't you make up with your dad? It's been years, and you probably don't even remember why, do you, Carl?" Lucy reminded, "It was over nothing, over a few cross words . . . I was there, remember? My parents are gone. if they were here, you know that they would help us."

"I know," Carl quietly confirmed. While Carl thought back over the matter of his relationship with his father, Lucy continued, "You're too proud. Carl. I know better than anyone, and you would let us suffer as a result of the grudge you have with your father."

Carl insisted, "There's a way out of this predicament, Lucy. We just have to figure it out," he reasoned.

Lucy returned, "Sometimes charity is the only way out."

Carl sat, taking it in, and after a pause, he defended, "I don't want handouts, Lucy. You can understand that, right?"

"Me neither . . . how about just a little help? Something to get us on our feet again?" Lucy agreed.

"I'll think about it," Carl resigned.

"I'll pray about it, Carl," Lucy added.

"You know prayin' don't put food on the table, Lucy. Besides, it's our problem, not God's, and we got ourselves here in the mess we're in. It's up to us to find a way out, don't you think?" Carl laid out.

Lucy reminded, "You told me to have faith in the doctor. I'm asking for you to have a little faith in God . . . and yes, Carl, he helps those who help themselves," Lucy aligned with Carl.

Carl offered, "Look on the bright side, Lucy."

"What bright side?" Lucy queried.

"Things to be thankful for, like we're together, and if we were working, we couldn't stay home with Mark. How about things could be worse than they are? Okay, we won't go there," Carl quickly rescinded, and amorously offered, "You know I love you, Lucy."

"I know, Daddy, I know," Lucy returned. "You know, Carl you used to believe in the magic of Christmas. You used to a long time ago. Don't you believe in anything?" Lucy engaged.

"I was a fool," Carl said flatly. Backing off his earlier statement, Carl finally conceded and, looking out the window, answered, "To tell you the truth, I don't know what I believe anymore."

"What about Bill?" Lucy reminded.

"What about him?" Carl followed.

"We're so focused on Mark and everything else, we treat him like he doesn't matter, like he doesn't even exist. He still believes in

Christmas magic. So do I. I guess that makes us fools as well, and we owe him that, Carl."

"I know," Carl finished.

Lucy gently delivered, "You realize Christmas is in three days. We have to give him something, at least a Christmas tree. We've never not had a Christmas tree, Carl." Lucy explained to Carl that it wasn't so much about the tree as it was about what the tree represented, in a word, hope, not to mention it was the one form of normalcy the struggling family could possibly afford.

The following day, while Carl was out looking for work, Lucy was sitting, quietly contemplating the couple's bleak future if things didn't improve soon, when there came a knock at the door. Lucy cracked the door to find a well-dressed man in a suit. He questioned, "Is this the Rosenthal household?" Lucy identified herself, "I am Lucy Rosenthal."

"I have an envelope for you here."

Lucy opened the door and cautiously received the envelope he presented to her, answering his greeting of merry Christmas. She thanked the gentleman; he tipped his hat, turned, and left her company expeditiously. She closed the door as she looked at the envelope, which had the word *gift* written on it in bold red foil. Lucy sat down and quickly opened the envelope, which contained a gift certificate for $141 redeemable at their local grocery market. A handwritten note at the bottom of the certificate read, "From someone who cares."

When Carl returned to the house that day, Lucy met him at the door and spoke excitedly, "Guess what, honey . . . I have a surprise."

"Really."

"Yes, just look."

Carl looked at the certificate Lucy presented and looked back at Lucy in surprise. "That's a lot of money . . . curious amount. I wonder who it's from."

Lucy repeated what was written, "From someone who cares . . . someone who cares about us, Carl."

Carl just looked at her amazed. Lucy went on to tell Carl the story of the well-dressed man who had come to the door and delivered the gift.

"Have you ever seen him before?"

"Never."

"Hmm," Carl puzzled. "I have some good news as well," Carl offered and went on, "I found someone to fix the car. He said we could pay him after the holidays."

"And that's not all," Lucy followed with the volley of good news. "I also received a card from the landlord today."

Expecting more bad news, Carl jested, "Let me guess, an eviction notice."

"You're wrong . . . he is passing us on the rent for December."

Carl was silent and sat down.

"Did you hear what I said? He is skipping the rent for December."

"What about October, and November, we haven't paid him for?"

"I told him we were going through some hard times right now—"

Carl interrupted, "Honey, I told you—"

"I know," Lucy volleyed. "I wasn't specific. He understood, Carl. He said we can catch up as we are able, isn't that great? It's happening."

Carl reflected, "I wonder what got into him."

Lucy called out, "Christmas . . . what else could it be?"

Carl added his sentiment, "Hearts are truly turned during this season, aren't they, Lucy?"

Lucy nodded excitedly and smiled and threw herself happily into Carl, and they held each other. While the family's many trials came in waves upon them, a tide of blessings moved in as well. And they rejoiced in this, and Lucy thanked God for his generosity.

And before they knew it, Christmas Eve was upon them, and in order to fulfill a promise he made to Lucy, "that Christmas would surely visit Bill," father and son set out in search of Christmas. With hope in his heart, the turning tide, and with Lucy behind him, Carl took the little boy by the hand. "What do you say we go find Christmas and bring it home to Mom?"

Lucy bent down and gently kissed the little boy. "Go with Daddy and find us a Christmas tree."

"I will, Mom," Bill assured his mother as he pulled his father out the door, and hand in hand the two travelers headed out into the cold night with the hope of performing a little Christmas magic of their own.

Carl drove into the night, and in the back of his mind, he pondered the thought of spending money he didn't have. Yet encouraged, he allowed his thought a voice, "Surely they would discount the trees on Christmas Eve . . . or give them away . . . or maybe even abandon them . . . don't you think so, Bill? Anyway we can always hope," he answered himself. Carl looked down at Bill sitting next to him, put his hand on his head, and smiled, "Don't want to let your mom down, that's for sure."

Empowered with the authority given to him by the spirit of Christmas, Bill stated firmly, "Don't worry, Dad, I know we'll find a tree. It's not too late, Dad." Carl smiled at Bill's confidence.

As Carl passed the lot where they normally went to get their tree in years past, Bill rose up out of his seat and exclaimed, "There's our tree, Dad!" He turned back to Carl and pointed. "See it—it's the only one left," the little boy heralded.

Carl slowed down and confirmed, "I see it." He further offered, "But maybe there's more to choose from at the other lot across town."

Bill settled back down in his seat and lamented. Bill posed, "Dad?"

"Yes, Bill," his dad joined.

"What if they don't have any there, Dad?"

Carl slowed the car, pulled over to the side of the road, and stopped. He looked down at the gas gauge, which was trending dangerously low; he then looked at Bill and suggested, "Maybe you're right, Bill. Maybe we get there, and there aren't any."

Bill added perspective as he forwarded, "That's our tree back there, Dad."

"You know, Bill, I believe you may be right," Carl considered, as he swung the car around and expeditiously headed back to the lot. Carl recommitted, assuring he would not go home empty-handed. As they drove up to the lot, Bill perked up, and together they focused on the one remaining tree standing alone in the center of the lot. The tree was illuminated, reflecting the glowing light emanating from the flickering flames rising up out of a burn barrel nearby.

Carl quickly parked, and Bill excitedly jumped out of the car. Carl called out after him, "Don't get ahead of yourself, son, and wait for Dad."

Bill ran around the car and grabbed his dad's hand and pulled him along, anxious to make their claim on the one and only tree left. Expecting that someone would be attending the fire in the burn barrel, Carl and Bill cautiously walked onto the lot, which appeared to be deserted.

"Where is everyone, Dad?" Bill asked his father.

"I don't know, son, I guess they all left," Carl answered, as he continued to look around for signs of life.

Bill added, "But it's Christmas, Dad."

Carl called out, "Anyone here?" and received only silence in return. They walked up to the abandoned tree and examined it closely. Looking down at Bill, Carl noted, "I don't know, Bill, it's pretty big and kinda scraggly, no wonder it was left here."

Not taking his eyes off the tree, Bill beamed, "I like it . . . it's perfect, Dad."

"Then I guess you should have it." Since Carl couldn't locate anyone, he decided to take the tree. Just as he placed his hands on it, a deep voice came out of the shadows; a large corpulent man emerged to join them in the glowing light. Startled, Carl quickly put a hand on Bill's shoulder, and the two drew back and faced the approaching man behind the booming voice.

The man, who looked older than he was, had a full beard, white as snow. He was dressed in a red flannel shirt with broad bright green suspenders holding up his worn and tattered blue jeans. He wore high laced faded black leather hiking boots into which his pant legs were stuffed. Carl thought the man looked a bit out of character for a hobo, as he was questionably fashionable, yet festive.

In an old, deep commanding voice, he spoke, addressing Bill, "Yes, I believe this tree is waiting for someone . . . just like you, young man." He then faced Carl and asked him straightaway, "You gonna pay for that tree . . . or just take it?"

"It was . . ." Carl stammered and started again, "I was just looking."

"Well, you're looking at it, only one left between here and . . . well between here and the North Pole, I suspect," the voice commanded.

Carl went on, "I didn't know there was anyone around. I thought the tree was abandoned." Turning his attention to the tree, Carl continued, "Thought we'd give it a home."

The two men stood there, each studying the other in the cold night air. Carl noticed that the man's face was weathered and deeply furrowed, fraught with lines of time. His cheeks, which rode high on his face, were flushed red from the cold, and the flickering firelight from the burn barrel danced upon their shiny surface. His eyes were icy blue, bright, and they glistened in the light.

Getting down to business, the man agreed, "Absolutely, it should have a good home and now. Do you have any money, friend?"

"Little to none," Carl offered honestly.

"None . . . hmm . . . seems we have something in common. You have holes in your trousers too?" He chuckled as he thrust his hands deep into his pockets, wiggling his fingers that protruded out through his tattered jeans. Getting back to the negotiation, the man asked Carl, "Then how in the world do you expect to pay for the tree?"

Although they never breached the subject, Carl suspected the old man had moved in after the owners of the lot had moved out and was now trying to make some money on the deal. Carl considered that he needed the tree, apparently as much as the man needed money, and so he engaged him civilly. "I'll give you all I have. How much do you want?"

"Well . . ." he stroked his heavy beard as he eyed Carl, sizing him up as it were. He continued, "Since you know it's the last Christmas tree anywhere, and since it is Christmas, and I'm in a generous mood, I'll give you a deal, a Christmas Eve special—it's a steal at ten dollars."

"What!" Carl bolted.

"But," in considering the boy, the man assured, still fishing for money, "I'll give it to you for . . . say, five dollars . . . and I'll even help you load it up. How's that sound to you?"

Carl went fishing for money. "I'll see what I have, and it's not much, if any . . . like I said."

"Not even $1.41? Which under the circumstances, I would consider," the man proposed.

Looking incredulously at the man, Carl reached deep into his pockets and swept up what was residing there in the lining. Carl turned out his pockets and opened his palm, and he counted aloud, "One crumpled up one-dollar bill, three dimes, and two nickels." Surprised, Carl pointed out, "Well, sir, you were close, very, very close." Carl paused and considered, "But how did you manage to guess . . . ?" And just then, something shiny on the ground caught Bill's eye, and he immediately swooped down and picked up a single penny. Bill presented his find to his father, "Look, Dad, here . . . I found a penny." Bill placed it in his dad's open hand, as Carl finished counting, "And one cent . . . making . . ."

"One dollar and forty-one cents," the stranger pointed out, sporting a wide grin.

"Exactly," Carl marveled in amazement and locked on the eyes of the sly old fox, all the while wondering how the man had performed that magic trick.

And to Carl's further amazement, the man seemed to answer his thoughts with, "Oh . . . you were wondering how . . . funny how that works, uh . . . well, I get lucky sometimes . . . although," he leaned forward slightly and quietly confided, "I'll tell you a secret. I also hear hearts and read minds." As he did so, the old man removed his glove and held out his hand to receive the money. Referring to his claim of reading minds and such, Carl jested, "And I'm afraid to ask how much that costs." The old man laughed jovially. "It's a clever trick, I'll give you that," Carl spoke as he placed the meager amount into the man's hand.

"Oh . . . I don't do tricks," the man instructed.

"Or whatever you call it then," Carl finished.

Upon consummation of their agreement and a firm handshake, the man grinned widely and offered, "It would seem the number 141 is your lucky number. The tree's all yours."

As Carl reached for the tree, unable to contain his excitement, Bill grabbed the tree, which was twice as big as he was, at same time as his dad. "Can I carry the tree, Dad, please . . . ? I can do it, Dad," his little boy assured.

The man intervened at that point and coaxed the tree from Bill and assured, "Here, let me get that for you, son. It's a little heavy and awkward."

Trusting the man's intention, Bill reluctantly let go of the tree, as the man lifted the tree high in the air and placed it on his broad shoulder, and in a warm deep bass voice, he began to sing the old traditional Christmas carol, "God Rest Ye Merry Gentlemen."

When they had put the tree into the trunk of the car, Carl turned toward the man and warmly thanked him. "Merry Christmas," Carl proclaimed.

"Merry Christmas!" Bill followed.

"And a very merry Christmas to you and your family, and a special blessing on the little one," the man happily returned.

Somewhat stunned at what this man seemed to know about this particular detail of his family, not knowing exactly what to say, Carl closed, "Come on, son. Let's go home, shall we?"

Now as Bill, happy about his prize tree, jumped up in the front seat of the car, Carl hesitated. He leaned on the open door of the car. In a state of reflection, Carl looked back at the man and pondered a thought, and Bill offered, "Can we take Santa Claus home with us too, Dad?"

Surprised, Carl looked at Bill and smiled. "You read my mind."

Bill quickly followed, "Can we, Dad? Please."

Carl explained, "He's not like a toy or something you can just pick up, take home, and play with."

"I know, Dad. I was just thinking . . . I just wanted to show Mom . . . and I like him."

"I know, Bill . . . he seems nice enough, but we don't know any-thing about him, really," his dad cautioned. Returning his attention to the man, Carl charged, "I'm pretty sure he's not Santa Claus, Bill. However . . ." he conceded, "he sure does look like him, doesn't he?" Further studying the man, Carl conceded, "He's just a man . . . a very clever man trying to make it in this life, trying to do more with less. You know, Bill, I do like the idea though." He closed the door and told Bill, "Just wait here, I'll be back in a moment."

"Where you going, Dad?" Bill called after him. Remembering his promise to bring Christmas home, Carl mulled over in his mind how happy it would make Lucy, *I'll not only bring a tree home, I'll bring Santa Claus home too.* Carl announced, "I'll be right back, son. There's something I have to do."

Bill looked on as his father walked back toward the man and joined him at the burn barrel, where he stood warming his hands. When Carl arrived at the fire, he reached out his hands to touch the fire's warmth. And for a time, occasionally glancing at each other, the two stared into the fire and watched as the glowing embers rose high into the air, dancing, crackling, and popping before they burn out and disappeared in the air. Carl finally broke the silence between the two with, "So . . ."

"So . . ." the man repeated.

"Kind of cold out here tonight . . ." Carl continued to beat about the bush as he looked up into the night sky and beheld the stars. "Beautiful but cold."

"Yep, a little frosty," the man agreed.

"Lots of stars."

"Indeed," the man joined as he looked up and scanned the heavens.

Carl questioned, "I was wondering . . . where will you go? I mean, with it being Christmas Eve and all?"

The man glanced over his shoulder at the bedroll lying under a makeshift lean-to in the shadows behind him. "I'll just lie down here, under the stars."

Concerned, Carl pointed out, "Oh . . . you'll freeze out here."

"In case you hadn't noticed, I was made for the cold. The creator was more than generous when he gave me this," he said as he patted his large, round, rotund belly. "Besides, I'm prepared." He pulled back his heavy overcoat.

"Yes, I can see that," Carl affirmed. Another moment passed, and Carl followed, taking a chance, not knowing the man but feeling like he could trust him, "I was wondering . . . my son thinks that you're Santa Claus."

"Oh, he does, does he? Well, my friend, what do you think about that?"

Carl just stared at the grinning man and wondered. With a big smile on his face, the man gently instructed, "We're all Santa Claus in our own way. He represents joy and exemplifies the very nature and spirit of giving . . . can't imagine a world without that."

"Suppose you're right, hadn't thought of it that way," Carl reflected. Carl interrupted the moment with, "I would . . . would you like to come home with us . . . for dinner with our family tonight? I mean of course, if you don't have anything else to do or friends . . ." Carl further stumbled along the rocky verbal path he chose to go down. "I mean that you . . . well, of course you have friends."

The man chuckled. "I know what you mean, and you don't have to explain yourself. I actually have a lot to do tonight. It's a very busy night for me, and FYI, I have friends all over the world."

Carl went along with the guise by the man pretending to be Santa Claus and jested, "Right, presents to deliver and all that."

"Yes," the man agreed, chuckled, and finished, "and all that."

Carl came back around to the subject of dinner, as he asked, "How about that invitation to dinner . . . huh . . . just realized I don't know your name."

The man answered, "Well, you could call me Santa Claus . . . or, my friends just call me Chris."

"My name is Carl, and my son's name is—"

"Bill," Chris finished.

"That's right . . . but how did you . . . ?" knowing that he hadn't mentioned his name to Chris before, Carl thought, looking back at the car where his son was patiently waiting.

"I heard you say his name earlier." Chris covered and continued, "So, a hot meal, dinner . . . a man's got to eat."

Carl smiled, "Yes, he does."

Chris went on, "Never turned down a home-cooked meal."

"I can see that," Carl followed. They both laughed jovially, and Chris added in a serious, genuine manner, "Yes, I would be happy to join you and your family for dinner. I would ask that you bring me back here promptly after dinner."

"Of course," Carl assured.

"Then let's be off," Chris directed.

Upon arriving at the car, Carl introduced Chris to Bill, "This is my son Bill."

Chris reached out his hand and warmly shook the hand of Bill. "Well, it's a pleasure to make your acquaintance, young man."

Bill beamed as he entertained the idea of actually taking the man he considered to be Santa Claus home for Christmas.

Carl went on to suggest, "Bill, why don't you get out and climb in back . . . and let Chris sit up front."

But before he could finish, Chris had already piled into the back seat with, "It's quite all right . . . I'm fine Carl."

On the way home to dinner, Carl apologized, "Look, I am sorry for your poverty, Chris, and I don't want you to get the wrong idea about coming to dinner . . . to think of it as charity or anything like that."

Putting things in perspective, Chris clarified calmly, "First, I'm not the one looking to steal . . ." and considering the boy, Chris restated, "I mean, take the last Christmas tree in the lot, because you don't have the money to pay for it." Chris paused momentarily before he continued, and in the space of that moment, Carl thought on Chris's words and admitted, "Of course you are right, Chris. I hadn't thought of it like that before."

Chris went on, "You know, Carl, that charity is a way to show love to your fellow man. It is an opportunity to positively affect the life of another. Oh, man, make no mistake," Chris upheld, "I am not poor by any means. I am friend to many all around the world, and many depend on what I bring to this world."

On the short ride home, Carl couldn't take his eyes off the strange yet familiar man looking back at him in the rearview mirror, comfortably seated in the back seat of the car, and he directed, "You look familiar to me, Chris. I know it sounds crazy, but I really feel like I know you." Carl just couldn't shake the feeling that he had known this man all along, and he inquired, "Have we met, Chris?"

Bill quickly turned around, getting up on his knees, flung his arms up over the seat and faced the man, and after momentarily studying him, matter-of-factly observed, "I think you're Santa Claus . . . you look just like Santa Claus, and you know stuff."

Chris chuckled and jested, "I've been called many things, just don't call me 'late for dinner.' My name is Chris, young master, and you are a very perceptive young man." And they filled the car with the merriment of laughter.

The thought persisted in Carl's mind that Chris may very well be no more than a very smart, clever man who, under his influence, made people somehow feel warmer, happier inside, and he knew that his family and their home could certainly use some of the that about now. He felt like he could trust him. There was something calming and comfortable about this benevolent soul. And Carl all the while balanced his impression of the stranger with reality, knowing that one could not be too careful when it came to strangers. On the other hand, in the past, Carl had brought home questionable characters to the dismay of his wife, and he wasn't absolutely sure how his decision to bring this man home would be received.

As though he was reading his mind, Chris observed, "I know it's hard to trust people these days. You just have to trust your senses and have faith."

"Not much to go on," Carl answered, studying Chris in the rearview mirror.

Chris explained, "Most of the time, it's all we've got, Carl. When you project light, you attract people. Don't doubt yourself. People who dwell in the shadows cannot survive in the light and will ultimately be revealed for who and what they really are." The wisdom and the truth of what Chris was saying hit Carl in a very personal way, continuing to melt his waning inhibitions about Chris.

When they arrived at the house, Lucy and Mark, who was warmly bundled in a blanket in her arms, anxiously met Carl, Bill, and the stranger at the door. As Carl was getting ready to introduce their guest, Bill jumped in and confidently delivered, "This is Santa Claus, Mom! We found him at the Christmas tree lot."

They all laughed, and Carl finished, "Honey, this is our friend Chris. This is my wife, Lucy, and Mark, the littlest of the clan."

"And certainly the most precious," Chris warmly observed.

Carl went on to tell Lucy, "Chris helped us with our tree, and I have invited him . . . to share Christmas dinner with us. Look, before you say anything, I know how it looks. It's a little awkward, I know, springing this on you at the spur of the moment and all, but —"

Chris intervened, humbly removed the red wool cap from his head, graciously bowed, and extended his hand out to Lucy insisting, "It's a pleasure to meet you, Lucy, and this precious angel," indicating the bundle of joy wrapped in her arms.

"Mark," Lucy introduced.

"Of course, Mark," Chris repeated, and continued, "What a blessing children are."

And Mark, seemingly aware of the attention given him, responded with a smile of approval. "He likes you, Chris," Lucy confirmed.

Chris turned to Lucy and considered, "I hope I'm not intruding."

To Carl's surprise, Lucy followed, "It's okay, Chris, of course you're welcome to join us. It's Christmas, and . . ." she added, "I was expecting you."

Carl smiled at his wife, pulled her to the side, leaned into her, and quietly inquired, "What do you mean you expected him?"

Lucy returned happily to Carl, "I expected you to bring home Christmas, and you did." She confirmed this with a smile and favored him with a kiss on the cheek. And so, with little Mark cradled in one arm, Lucy took Chris by the hand and led him into the house followed by Bill and Carl.

The family immediately sat down to dinner, and Chris gave a most eloquent blessing over the meal and their family. They laughed and ate their fill and raised their glasses high into the air and toasted Christmas. At the completion of the most satisfying dinner, Chris complimented Lucy on the wonderful meal she had prepared. Lucy thanked him, adding that their family was happy they were able to share it with him. Lucy told Chris that she had to share the compliment with the giver of an anonymous gift they had received quite unexpectedly, enabling them to buy the food for the meal. Chris inspiringly confirmed, "Then we are all blessed."

With a most satisfying dinner concluded, they all retired to the living room and proceeded to meticulously decorate the Christmas tree, which they had earlier set up in a place of prominence by the fireplace. They sang all of the Christmas carols of old, and they talked of many things that night and shared each other as friends. With uncommon authority, Chris talked about his many brothers and the importance of family and friends. He went on to discuss the meaning and the magic of Christmas, of the spirit of giving, of love and faith. He recounted the ageless story of the first Christmas when Jesus was born—God's glorious gift to the world. When the night finally came to a close, Lucy put little Mark, who was fast asleep deep in the overstuffed chair by the fire, to bed. A short time later, after returning to the warmth of the living room, she turned her attention toward Bill and announced that it was his bedtime. After a slight protest, not wanting to miss anything, Bill finally surrendered and bade his mom and dad good night. And bestowing a special farewell greeting to their guest, Bill stopped in front of Chris and looked long at him, reached up, wrapped his little arms around his neck, and quietly spoke into his ear, "Merry Christmas. I know you're Santa Claus."

Chris hugged him back and returned, "Merry Christmas to you, son." And off to bed the little boy trotted, with a headful of dreams and his faith in Christmas restored. On his way, Bill stopped and turned and added one more observation, "Santa . . . I mean, Chris, you smell good, like Christmas trees and peppermint," and with that, he scurried off to bed, and they all laughed long and hard. Now for their son to greet a friend he'd only just met in this manner was extremely unusual and extraordinary to watch.

Bill was convinced that he had indeed spent Christmas Eve with the one man that made all the Christmas magic happen for all children young and old, and there was no doubt in his mind that this man was none other than the real Santa Claus. It was the Christmas that Bill's gift wasn't a toy or a trinket you could touch; it wasn't a present he could possess. It didn't come in a box, wrapped with foil and ribbons and bows. It was a timeless gift—the gift of happiness and of joy. It was a spiritual gift passed from one to another, a gift that he would treasure all his life.

And when it came time for Chris to leave their company, he thanked Lucy heartily and warmly hugged her, as if they were old friends. Not wanting the night to end yet understanding that Chris had to go, Lucy reluctantly released her hold on him and profusely thanked him and wished him a merry Christmas. Lucy added, "You know, Chris, Bill is right. You do smell like pine and peppermint."

Chris simply grinned and replied, "Christmas trees and peppermint tea—gives me away every time." They laughed and Chris bade her good night.

Carl returned Chris to the place he had picked him up. Carl slowly pulled up to the lot, stopped the car, turned to Chris and offered his hand, which Chris took in his, and he thanked him. "Merry Christmas, Chris, thank you . . . for everything. You have given me and my family hope and happiness and brought so much joy into Bill's life."

Chris returned, "It is I who are blessed by you and your family. You validate what I know about the human spirit . . . thank you." The two nodded to each other, and Chris got out of the car, briefly hesitating at the door; he reached back in and presented a sealed envelope to Carl. "Oh, I almost forgot to give this to you."

"What is it?" Carl asked.

"Please give it to Lucy. She'll know what to do with it," Chris assured.

Looking at him questioningly, Carl affirmed, "Yes, I'll give it to her, but . . ."

Chris added, "You are a good man, Carl. You have a good heart, and you and your family deserve the very best."

Carl spoke once more, "Chris . . ."

"Yes, Carl," Chris returned.

"Are you Santa Claus?"

Chris just smiled warmly and answered, "I am just a man like you, a man who cares about the welfare of others." Chris knew that Carl had one more question for him, and so he patiently waited for Carl to finish.

"Where will you go, Chris?"

Chris quietly answered, "Where I'm needed." And with that, he gently closed the door of his car and disappeared into the silvery shadows. Carl watched him as he walked away and spoke a thought, *Goodbye, my friend, until we meet again.*

Chris was warm and captivating, and in his presence, Carl and Lucy forgot all about their troubles. It was as if they didn't seem to matter anymore and that everything they had been going through would melt away and things would be okay.

When Carl returned home from dropping Chris off at the Christmas tree lot, to his delight, Lucy met him at the door. She embraced Carl and led him into the living room where they sat down together in front of the fire and the Christmas tree. The mood was light, and their home was happy. Smiling, Lucy offered, "I don't know why exactly, but I feel really good and warm inside, like a heavy weight has been lifted off me. I'm actually looking forward to the future and not dreading it. I'm excited to be alive."

"Me too . . . I feel young," Carl joined and continued, "by the way, Chris gave me this to give to you." He pulled the envelope out of his pocket that Chris had given him.

"What's this?" Lucy wondered.

"A Christmas present perhaps . . . I don't know," Carl conjectured and added, "He said you would know what to do with it."

Lucy took the sealed envelope and quickly opened it. She sat speechless, with a look of astonishment on her face.

"What is it, Lucy?" Carl entreated.

"It's a list of five wishes," Lucy said, surprised.

"Wishes . . . for what?" Carl followed.

"They are wishes that I made for us," Lucy answered.

"But . . . how did . . . ?" Carl figured.

"You mean . . . how did he get it . . . how did he know?" Lucy finished and contemplated the mystery. "But he couldn't have known . . . unless he really was . . ."

"Santa Claus," Carl completed her thought.

"Or . . . an angel," Lucy resolved as she sat back deep into the couch. They just looked at each other incredulously and wondered how it could be.

Carl picked up the wish list she had laid in her lap and read it. Lucy told Carl the whole story from the beginning of what she had done, and he listened intently to her tale. "A couple of weeks ago, when things were looking really bad for us, I made a list of five wishes, things I prayed for. I was desperate to get help for us in any way possible, Carl, from anyone who would listen. There was no other way, and I prayed and believed that if I had enough faith, I would be heard and my wishes would come true, and that our troubles would somehow magically disappear. After I made the list, I put it in a blank envelope and sealed it. But what I don't understand is that it appears that the envelope was never opened."

"Until now," Carl followed.

Lucy nodded, adding, "Yes, until now."

Carl held up the list and envelope, indicating, "And this is the list?"

"Yes," Lucy confirmed with a nod. Lucy continued, "After I wrote it and sealed it in an envelope, I wasn't sure what to do with it. I went to the church and left the envelope on a table inside the foyer. As I walked back out to the car, I changed my mind and took it back. I ultimately decided to mail it to—"

"Let me guess . . . to Santa Claus," Carl finished.

Lucy quickly revealed, "Look, Carl, I know it sounds crazy . . . childish in fact. I was scared, and I didn't know what else to do!"

"No . . . no, are you kidding? It's not crazy at all," Carl comforted as he wrapped her tightly in his arms and assured her, "I love you for it. I am glad you did it."

Lucy pulled away a little and spoke, "It was real then, it really happened. A miracle happened to us, Carl."

"Well, I think it's a little beyond coincidence. It would seem your prayers have been answered . . . your wishes granted." They were giddy and laughed out loud, embracing and exchanging "I love yous" and thanking God for all that had happened.

As Lucy and Carl celebrated, Carl stopped short as he pointed out, "Lucy, wait, honey, wait a minute."

"What is it?" Lucy said, concerned.

"It's probably nothing . . ."

"What?" Lucy insisted.

"Well . . ." Carl revealed as he studied the list, "look here, at your first wish. There's no check mark on that one, while all the other wishes are checked."

"Here, let me see it," Lucy insisted and read her first wish aloud. "I would give anything if you would only spare the life of my son, but Mark is fine, Carl." Lucy's heart began to race, and she jumped up and immediately ran back to the back bedroom where her son was sleeping peacefully, scooped him up, and brought him out to Carl. They both examined the boy as he woke up, looked at them, and smiled and cooed, quite contentedly.

"Thank God," Lucy sighed.

Carl questioned, "I wonder what it means."

"Don't know, Carl, but our beautiful boy is healthy, he's fine."

"I think you got all your wishes regardless, Lucy," Carl confirmed.

"Yes, we did, Carl . . . yes, we did. I love you."

"I love you," Carl finished.

Later that night, unable to sleep, excited about the remark-able events of the previous day, anxiously awaiting the dawning of Christmas Day, Lucy lay awake on her bed, staring at the digital clock on her night stand. It wasn't the digital display emanating a soft red glow; it was the number 1:41 that flashed before her eyes that caught her attention just then. "One forty-one," Lucy spoke aloud, breaking the silence. She focused on the number and was transfixed by it. Again she repeated, "One forty-one."

"What, Lucy?" Carl stirred.

Lucy turned toward Carl and asked a question that she was try-ing to reconcile in her mind. "The number is 141 . . . Carl, it just popped into my head."

"What do you mean . . . the number is 141?"

"The time is 1:41." Lucy raised herself up on her elbows, moved in close to Carl, and continued, "Remember the gift certificate was

$141. Don't you think that's an odd number? I was thinking why not 140 or 150? And I just happened to look at the clock at the very moment it turned 1:41."

Carl lay there thinking about it while Lucy, who was suspended above him, waited for him to say something. After a moment, Carl linked, "You know, Lucy, maybe you're on to something."

Mistaking Carl's reply as patronizing, Lucy lay back down and stared into the darkness and resigned, "I know what you're thinking. It's a coincidence, and I'm making something out of nothing. You're probably right."

Carl came back, "No, Lucy, there may be something more to it." Carl continued, "You know, talking about odd numbers, guess how much I paid for the Christmas tree?"

"What did you pay? You never told me," Lucy reminded.

Carl said, "You're not going to believe it$1.41. I thought it was a little strange at the time, but that's all the money I had . . . I mean, Bill and I had . . . I had $1.40, and Bill just happened to find a penny on the ground, making the amount—"

"One dollar and forty-one cents," Lucy finished.

"One forty-one," Carl repeated.

Lucy broke the silence again with, "Maybe it's our lucky number, Carl."

"Maybe," Carl said with reservation, as he recalled what Chris had said to him at the Christmas tree lot when he gave him the money for the tree (that "it would seem the number 141 is your lucky number").

Moving beyond the numerical paradox, and nevertheless satisfied, Lucy quietly reflected, "I got my wishes and the answer to my prayers."

"It would seem so, Lucy," Carl agreed.

"One thing that puzzles me though," Lucy offered.

"What's that, Lucy?" Carl followed.

"Who do you think he was—an angel, Santa Claus, God, or a wizard or what?"

"Or what," Carl answered and provided, "I think the ultimate force that guides all life goes by many names and titles. I believe he was an agent of God."

Lucy finished, "One thing I know for sure . . . there is more than meets the eye to this life and this world . . . and miracles do happen."

"Yes, they do, Lucy . . . yes they do," Carl agreed.

And so it was that Lucy incidentally got everything on her wish list. The following year, exactly 141 days into her pregnancy with a baby girl, Lucy unfortunately had a miscarriage, sadly losing her unborn daughter. At that time, either by chance or by choice, Lucy failed to connect the incident to the wishes she had made or the encounter with their visitor on that one eventful Christmas Eve the previous year. Lucy and Carl would not be spared from facing the truth for long as they were reminded that following Christmas.

One day when Lucy was home alone, going through a box of Christmas cards and keepsakes in preparation for Christmas the following year, she inadvertently uncovered the wish list she had saved from the previous Christmas. She again read the words she had written out of desperation the year before ("I would give *anything* if you would only spare the life of my son). And it was at that moment, as she read the first wish on the list aloud, that Lucy realized for the first time since her miscarriage the significance of what her wish cost her. Lucy's heart broke just then at the thought of what she had done, and she openly wept for the daughter who never was, for the daughter that she would never know in this life, and the daughter she wished away. And her tears fell onto the paper and could not wash away the writing of her hand, for she could not take back the wish once it had been granted. She realized she was faced with an impossible decision. And for a time, Lucy lived in sorrow and could not be comforted; ultimately it was time that was her friend and healed her broken heart and the love of her family who needed her that pulled her through, and finally her faith that gave her peace and restored her perspective on life. With a newfound sobriety, they now look back on their mixed blessing, and quietly reflect and privately assess the price of a wish and the cost of a prayer.

And the family moved on. They lived happily together, forgetting their past woes. And Lucy poured herself into her two boys, Bill and Mark, who grew up strong and became fine young men with families of their own; and Lucy and Carl, who were never closer, lived long and fruitful lives and had many more adventures along the way. They realized that nothing good comes in life without a cost, and they are reminded to be careful what you wish for, for you may get it.

(by Darrell W. McNabb, 2015)

About the Author

Darrell W. McNabb, who is otherwise referred to as D by those who know him, took up writing early in his teenage years in order to capture those compelling, fleeting impressions of life and save them for later reflection. Now much older and having lived many adventures, he has accumulated an extensive body of work, which includes numerous musical compositions, short stories, poetry, and a soon-to-be-released novel, in which he recounts the time he spent working as an undertaker in the funeral business. Thus far, Darrell has kept these many works relatively close to his chest and, for the past several years, has shared his collection of Christmas stories exclusively with his friends and family. Having been moved by these beautiful stories, they have pressed him to extend these uplifting tales to a wider audience. And so with the completion of his latest work, he will finally venture beyond the wheelhouse and share his passion for writing with all, as he offers this collection of heartwarming short stories, highlighting the Christmas season, inspired by the stirring accounts of those individuals who play out their parts in these pages.